Cakes and Killers

A Terrified Detective Mystery
Book 8

Carole Fowkes

Chapter One

I CLOSED MY APARTMENT door behind me and leaned against it. Home at last with my lovable pug, Charlie, the only male I could always depend on to be thrilled to see me. I squatted and gave him a hug, though it was hard to hold on to his wiggling form.

Preventing him from licking off all my makeup stopped me from thinking about my latest downer dating adventure. By the time I got Charlie's leash on for his walk and we were out the door, it came back to me. *Ugh.*

Anyone who thought modern dating was fun had to be delusional. This latest guy, Thomas, looked good in his photo, and he was an engineer, so he couldn't be a dummy. His emails and our phone conversations were pleasant. But someone must have given him a script for those. His allure didn't hold up in person.

I'd just sat through two hours of the dullest dinner

ever. Not only had he gone on about growing mushrooms in his basement, he then spent thirty minutes describing the various soils in which each type grew best. If it were possible to bore people to death, Thomas would make a great serial killer.

My cell phone was ringing when Charlie and I returned to my apartment. I groaned softly. My Aunt Lena who since my mother died, took it upon herself to oversee my life, was calling.

Without so much as a hello, she started, "So how was your date? What was his name, anyway?"

I slid down the wall until I was at the same height as Charlie, who took the opportunity to cram his head beneath my hand for an ear scratching. "Hi, Aunt Lena. His name is Thomas. It was just dinner, and that was fine."

"Fine, you have another date, or fine, you got through the meal and will never see him again?"

Ignoring Charlie's call for attention, I blew out a breath of air. "The latter, I hope."

"What'd you mean? Have you finally realized having three men in your life is two too many?"

I ignored her last question. "I might have been too nice. When he asked if I liked mushrooms, I should've said no."

"I don't know what mushrooms have to do with any-thing, but if you don't like him, don't lead him on." Her voice turned judgmental. "Don't do what you did with poor Brian." She was referring to my former fiancé, Cleveland Police Detective Brian Corrigan. No matter how often I tried explaining the breakup that occurred four months ago was for the best, she would just harrumph and continue laying the blame totally at my feet.

An unbidden memory drifted before me of that relationship with Corrigan. The attraction and hopes for our happy future were gone. I sighed, knowing I would probably grieve the loss for a long time.

Too tired to defend myself, I agreed. "You're right. If he asks me to go out again, I'll politely decline."

"What are you going to say?"

Since my aunt had married my assistant at DeNardo and Son Private Investigation, Ed Horwath, she was getting way too involved in my social life.

"Something will come to me." To my surprise, she didn't dig further. But she wasn't yet done with probing into my love life. "So, do you have another date with that old lawyer guy?"

I suppressed an annoyed sigh. "You mean Paul? He's not an old guy! He's only forty-three. That's just ten years older than me."

"Humph. Maybe it doesn't seem much older now, but if you stay with him, one day he'll be ninety, and you'll only be eighty." She said it with a *so-there* in her voice. "At least David is closer to your age. And a nice boy."

I sucked in a breath. I wasn't going to win any argument with my aunt concerning who I was seeing. Not since Brian and I ended our engagement. Thankfully, a call was coming in. It was David, the 'nice boy'. "Aunt Lena, I've got to take this. I'll catch you later." I switched over to the other call before my aunt could get out another snide comment. Adhering to the idea that someone can hear a smile through the phone, I plastered one on my face. "Hi, David! How are you?"

"Were you just talking to Lena?"

Dropping any pretense at being a ray of sunshine, I moaned. "How did you know?"

He chuckled. "Because my mom just called me. About you." David's mother, Angie, was Aunt Lena's dearest pal and assistant at my aunt's bakery, *Cannoli's*.

I didn't find this as humorous as David apparently did. "Did you explain that we're, you know, not having a thing?" The spark that had ignited between us in January had mellowed and turned into a solid, thoroughly enjoyable friendship. So, I was seeing other people, and I assumed he was too. But, at his request, we never talked about that.

Unbelievably, another call was coming in. "David, I'm sorry. I need to go." With a quick goodbye, I switched over to Paul, the lawyer.

I hoped he wasn't cancelling our plans for Sunday. He was taking me out on his sailboat. I was excited, having only been on Lake Erie once, and that had been on the dinghy my father had used for fishing.

In a deep baritone voice I imagined juries found commanding, Paul said, "Hi Claire, I'm glad I caught you. Listen, about sailing tomorrow. I have a last-minute conference call I have to be on in the morning. Would you mind meeting me at the club instead of me picking you up?"

"No, not at all. Do I need a code to get in and park?"

He gave me a set of four numbers. "That should do it. Claire, I'd like nothing better than to talk with you, but the chit-chat will have to wait until tomorrow. I'll be more relaxed." He did sound harried and his words came out as if they were balancing on a tightrope.

"Not a problem. See you tomorrow. Have a good eve—"

He was off the call before I could finish my sentence. I squinted at the phone, deciding Paul must be very busy. He was usually the pinnacle of courtesy. Shrugging, I scratched behind Charlie's ear once more, grabbed a glass of water and dropped onto the sofa for some television before bed.

ༀ

SUNDAY MORNING came quickly. My personal care and pet duties completed, I grabbed my new jacket that went with my recently purchased sailing outfit and hoped that I'd be warm enough. Even in early May, Cleveland weather isn't exactly balmy.

I made the trip to Lake Erie Yacht Club in fifteen minutes, so I was a little early. Paul followed a bit later, parked in the member's lot and came over to my car. Being about six feet tall, dark brown hair flecked with gray and green eyes that took a person's measure immediately, he looked every bit the successful lawyer. A smile drifted across my face. "Good morning, Paul."

His smile matched mine. "Hi yourself." He opened my car door for me. "I thought we'd start out the day with a light breakfast at the club. Sound good?"

I pressed my hand against my stomach to stifle its low growl. "Perfect."

With his hand on my back, he guided me toward the restaurant within the clubhouse, and the maître d, with his crisp white shirt and pressed trousers seated us.

Our server quickly made her way to us. "Good morning." She was bulky, but not fat, and didn't look a day over twenty-five. She gave us a bright toothy smile, her bobbed auburn hair catching the room's lights. "What can I get for you and your friend?"

Paul glanced her way. "Where's Brenda? She always waits on me."

Her smile disappeared. "I'm sorry, Mr. Morley. She called in sick, so I'm subbing for her."

"I hope she feels better." Without looking at the menu, he ordered. "We're sailing today, so we'll have the usual."

"I'm sorry. Nobody told me what that is." She cast her eyes downward, like a puppy that did its business where it shouldn't have. Paul glanced up at her, a frown on his face that evaporated as quickly as it formed. "No worries." He placed his order and practically waved her away.

He turned to me and confided, "Not only is Brenda a good waitress, she always manages to get me the best of whatever they're serving."

I nodded, wondering if Brenda provided him with

more than food and drink.

I didn't have long to ponder that question. Paul centered all his attention on me and began an amusing story about his elder child, Janette, and her first trip on a sailboat. He was in the middle of the tale when his phone rang. He scowled and held the phone against his chest. "My apologies, Claire. I have to take this call." He stepped away from the table and toward the entrance, where the waitress stood, shuffling through the menus.

I couldn't hear his conversation, but from his stiff pose, it was evident he didn't like what the caller was saying.

The food arrived just as Paul hustled back to our table. The control in his voice barely masked his anger. "Claire, something's come up." He motioned the waitress over. "We'd like our orders to-go please." Then he addressed me, "I hope you won't mind eating on the boat."

Paul's omelet and my lovely chocolate crepe were unceremoniously shoved into containers. Practically starving, I fought my desire to lick off all the whipped cream left on the plate. The server took Paul's credit card and disappeared to ring up our bill.

"I'll make this up to you, Claire. I promise." He lifted my hand, squeezed it, and gave me a dazzling smile.

I released a sigh and, in a playful turn, joked, "I'm warning you, Paul. Payback can be harsh."

The waitress, having returned to the table, cleared her throat. "Here you go, Mr. Morley."

Paul added a tip and scribbled his name on the bill.

"Let's go, Claire."

I had to move fast to keep up with him, finally speaking once we got outside. "Hey, if this is a race, I think you're winning."

"Sorry." He stopped and out of the side of his mouth, added dryly, "I seem to be apologizing a lot to you today. And yesterday."

He looked so sincere I had to take it easy on him. "It's really okay. We all have times like you're having today." I chuckled. "And yesterday."

Balancing the food containers in one hand, Paul leaned over and kissed me lightly on the cheek. "You're a delight, Claire. Thank you."

I smirked while my stomach grumbled. "Well, I won't be such a delight if I don't get to eat soon."

"Understood. And it would have been great to have breakfast in the restaurant, but someone uninvited was insisting on joining us. I couldn't have that."

Curiosity momentarily overtook my hunger pangs. "Oh, a colleague? Or a client?"

He waved his hand. "Doesn't matter. It's not worth ruining the rest of today over."

I didn't press, because we began walking down a pier toward a gorgeous docked sailboat. "Wow!" I stared at the huge vessel. "How many people can you have on this thing?"

"Right now, only two, you and me." He handed me the food. "If you'll take these, I'll board and then help you up."

I have to admit, he was much more graceful getting onto the ship. It took me a minute to get my sea legs.

"This is beautiful, Paul." A freezing breeze whipped through the boat and my thin jacket. I shivered.

"Come on. Let's go below to eat breakfast. It'll be warmer there. Afterwards, we'll take the boat out around the lake."

The ship's galley had a stove and storage space. A table with a settee that wrapped around its sides sat across from a small refrigerator. Paul pulled out a chilled bottle of champagne. "Thank you for being a good sport in leaving the restaurant. I hope this will make up for the delay in eating and the loss of ambiance." He took a knife from a drawer to cut the foil off the bottle and nodded toward a cabinet. "There're glasses in there."

Retrieving the stemware, I turned to Paul, ready for him to pour the bubbly. Then I heard a motor from another boat, rocking us and throwing me off balance and into Paul. I recoiled, but it was too late. The knife he was holding ripped through my jacket and tore into the inside of my lower left arm.

Fearing the worst, I lifted my appendage. The blade had created a bright red fissure in my skin. My breath caught. Rivulets of my blood spread across the light blue of my outfit. Luckily, I didn't see any muscle or even worse, bone.

"My God!" Paul dropped both the bottle and the knife and grabbed a towel to wrap around my arm, but the wound bled through the fabric.

I shook my head. "No, my fault." I cradled my bloody arm with my opposite hand, "I better go home."

"No, I'll take you to the emergency room. You may need stitches." His phone went off. "Dammit!"

I swallowed hard. "Answer it. It's okay." Sure, my searing pain wasn't important.

He glanced at the caller's name and said to the phone, "Oh, forget it." And swiped to decline the call. Back to me, he insisted, "I'll take you to the ER. No argument."

His phone rang once again. I swear the ringing was more insistent. What made it most annoying was that I knew he wanted to answer it.

Instead of knocking the phone out of his hand like I wanted to do, I stuck my chin out bravely and declared, "There's a doc-in-a-box down the street. I can get there by myself." Joan of Arc would've been proud of me.

I pressed the towel and my wounded arm against my chest and glanced at him, half-expecting him to protest more strongly against my going alone. Actually, wanting him to insist. He owed me that.

Instead, he took a step toward me and also answered his phone, yelling into it, "Give it a rest."

My arm was burning and throbbing at the same time, and now I was in no mood to wait for his phone call to end. I made my way up onto the deck.

Following me above board, his phone still in his hand, Paul insisted, "Don't be foolish, Claire. I'll take you."

Too late now, jerk.

Maybe I was being childish, but I kept going. I was

hurt, and, yes, a part of me would've liked him to come with me, but there were other considerations. I really didn't want to go to the emergency room. I carried minimal insurance, and no way could I afford the charges of a hospital emergency room. I sure didn't want this affluent lawyer to know I wasn't capable of paying a clinic bill. That I wasn't a successful businesswoman. DeNardo and Son was doing better than ever, but the overhead, operating expenses, and my modest living wage ate away at any extra money. My credit cards were just about maxed out. I'd foolishly spent more than I'd planned on my outfit for today. The outfit that was now ruined.

I took a deep, shaky breath. "It's fine, Paul. I think it stopped bleeding." It had done nothing of the kind. "I'll just go home and get out of these bloody clothes. I'll call you." The pain was making my knees weak. *I should forget my pride and let him take me. If he asks once more…*

He sighed heavily and glanced at his phone. "Make sure you call me as soon as you get home. And let me know how much it costs. I'll reimburse you."

So incensed I didn't trust myself to speak, I nodded, thinking that was the least he could do. He jumped onto the pier and gently helped me off the boat. Kissing my cheek, he returned to his phone.

The anger-fueled energy I'd felt upon leaving the boat, dissipated instantly. On legs that felt as if they were made of wet cardboard, I made my way down the pier and onto the paved parking lot. Concerned about how I'd drive myself with one arm, I didn't even notice the maître d from the restaurant until we almost collided.

He skidded to a stop and took in my appearance. "Ma'am, are you all right? Can I help?"

I shook my head. "I'm okay. Had a slight accident. I'm just driving myself to the clinic down the street." I paused. "You know, you could do something for me. Would you open my car door?"

"Okay, not a problem."

He helped me into my car and asked, "Anything else?"

He looked relieved when I thanked him and said, "That's it." I slumped against the seat and, gritting my teeth, I unwrapped the towel and examined my arm. I moaned, but at least the bleeding had let up a bit. Still, I knew that going to the urgent care place was a good idea. Especially since I'd insist Paul pay me back for the charges. I just hoped my credit card would cover it. If not, I'd have to call my father and beg.

Thank goodness the urgent care place was close by. I pulled up to the building perspiring and shivering at the same time. One look at my arm and the receptionist immediately placed me into one of the rooms.

Dr. Romansky and a nurse whose name I didn't catch cleaned and sutured my arm. To my amazement and thanks-be-to-God, my credit card accepted the charges. Before I left I had a sewn-up arm and a prescription for both pain pills and an antibiotic. This day had not turned out the way I'd expected, or hoped. Now, all I wanted to do was hide in bed under the covers.

But first, the drugstore. I didn't want to press my financial luck, but decided I'd better get both prescriptions filled. While I waited, I called Paul to tell him what he owed me. Other than that, I really didn't want to see him again. Ever. Any man who'd put his precious phone above a bleeding woman wasn't worth my time. My interest in him had waned with every stitch I received.

My call went straight to his voicemail. I debated on telling him how much to reimburse me, but I decided not to leave the amount in a message. "It's Claire. Call me back." I bit my lower lip in annoyance. He was probably still talking to whoever had insisted on speaking with him earlier.

Driving home was a little bit less of a challenge. I didn't have to worry about getting blood all over my car.

I finally made it into my apartment. Charlie, ordinarily an ecstatic-at-seeing-me jumper, must have sensed all was not well. When I opened the door, he sniffed and with barely a wag of his tail, dropped to his belly and let out a sorrowful whimper. I gave him a pat with my good arm. "Yeah, Charlie, I feel the same way."

He followed me into the kitchen and watched as I took my pills with some water. I wished other males were as empathetic as my dog. I changed out of my now destroyed outfit and into a tee shirt, tottered to the sofa and laid down, with Charlie at my feet. The last waking thought I had was how delicious that crepe at the yacht club had looked.

Chapter Two

THE FIRST THING I recalled when I woke up was Charlie's wet nose against the palm of my good hand. His tail wagged and I knew he wanted to go outside. I bent my head from left to right, hoping to get the kinks out and then stood. My left arm throbbed, but it wasn't time to take another pain pill yet.

It was still light outside, and the sun was shining. I guessed I'd slept for only a few hours. Grabbing my phone and hooking Charlie to his leash, we went down the stairs and out the apartment door.

We walked along the sidewalk in front of my building, and Charlie sniffed around, pulling me forward. I stood firm, though, and checked my phone. To my surprise and irritation, Paul hadn't returned my call.

I thought about ringing him again but decided to be a bit more patient. If I didn't hear from him first, I'd call Sunday morning.

Charlie, having done his duty, must have decided he was now hungry and tugged on his leash to get back inside. My stomach was rumbling, so I was happy to oblige.

I rustled up some left-over lasagna for me and beefy dog food for Charlie, and we returned to the sofa. It was four o'clock. I still had the evening, but my day had been disappointing, expensive, and painful.

Rather than sitting around moping, I decided to close out the file on my latest case. My client, John Alameda, was convinced his brother-in-law, Mike, was siphoning money from their laundry business. He didn't want to go to the police, probably because he wasn't squeaky clean himself.

After a couple hours, the ache in my left arm made working next to impossible, and I decided all I was fit to do was watch television. But first, another pain pill.

I turned on the local news and soon my eyelids drooped. I jerked awake, though, when I heard the perfectly coiffed newscaster announce, "A well-known Cleveland attorney was found dead in his boat. More details after the break."

I sat up ramrod straight and flicked the remote to another station. A serious, bespectacled weather forecaster was pointing to a band of showers, so I went back to the original news program. The newscaster appeared on screen just as someone began pounding at my door.

Trying to be heard over Charlie's barking, I shouted, "Go away. I don't want any." My eyes remained glued to the screen, but the insistent rapping drowned the newswoman's voice.

"Open the door, Claire. It's Brian."

My stomach dropped, flipping as it went on its way. Forcing my wooden legs to unfold, I scooted around Charlie, who was now leaping at the door. "I'm coming." My voice sounded as if someone was strangling me.

My mind raced. *What should I say?* I hadn't seen Corrigan since we ended our engagement. *Why now?* Of course, the murdered lawyer. *Had to be Paul.*

My fingers fumbled, but I finally succeeded in unlocking and opening my door.

There he was, as handsome as ever. Maybe more so. Next to him stood one of the reasons Corrigan and I had cancelled our engagement. It was his partner, the woman I unaffectionately refer to as the Mistress of Darkness, Abby Tilka. Grudgingly, I admitted they made a gorgeous couple. He with his light hair and blue eyes and she with raven hair, flawless skin and eyes that vied with Corrigan's for winner of the bluest-of-blue.

The scowl on Corrigan's face told me they weren't here on a social visit. I tried to keep my voice calm and in control. "What can I do for you officers?" It came out as high as if I'd sucked air in from a helium balloon.

Abby stepped forward and in a most officious tone declared, "Ms. DeNardo, you need to come down to the station with us to answer some questions."

Corrigan's face was unreadable, but I already knew the story. Still, I responded, "What's this about, Brian? Am I being arrested?"

"No, we just want some information about Paul Morley."

That newscaster had been talking about Paul. Still, I needed confirmation. "Why? Is Paul dead?"

Abby snarled, "You're going to answer our questions. And if you don't cooperate—"

Corrigan cut her threat short. "Don't make this harder than it is, Claire. Please."

I knew I didn't have a choice. To gain time and hopefully to get my head straight, I glanced down at my extra-long tee shirt. "Can I at least change clothes?" Believing Abby would have gladly handcuffed me and dragged me down to the station as I was, I looked at Corrigan, "I don't plan on escaping through the bedroom window."

He relaxed just a little. "Sure. We'll wait."

Abby added, "Inside."

Charlie let out one growl aimed at Abby. *Good boy, Charlie.* Then he wagged his tail and leapt at Corrigan. *Traitor.*

At least they didn't insist on me keeping the bedroom door open while I dressed. That bit of privacy gave me time to control my breathing.

Abbey was standing so close to the bedroom door, I almost bumped into her. Corrigan was squatting and playing with my dog.

"I'm ready." My voice was so shaky it revealed I was anything but.

I should've been asking a million questions on the way

to the police station, but my brain was so scrambled from the pain medication, I couldn't form the right sequence of words.

In no time, Corrigan and Abby had hustled me inside and into an interrogation room.

My mouth was dry, but I didn't want to ask for anything to drink. I knew how this worked. They'd probably keep the cup for DNA evidence.

Corrigan began. "Claire, what was your relationship with Paul Morley?" He was all serious professional now.

I folded my hands in front of me to stop them from shaking. "Why? There's not much to tell. We'd gone out a few times. That's it."

Abby leaned into me. "You were with him Saturday morning."

Sitting back to get some space between us, I answered, "He invited me for breakfast and then we were going sailing." My wounded arm ached. "But I had an accident and had to go home."

Corrigan loosened his tie. "Tell us about the accident, Claire."

My tongue felt as if it was glued to the roof of my mouth. "Paul was trying to open a bottle of Champagne with a knife. I bumped into it. Why? What does it matter?" *Wake up, Claire. It matters to them.* "You can't possibly believe I had anything to do with Paul's death!"

Before I got an answer, somebody knocked on the door. Corrigan answered it and stepped outside. I could only hear muffled voices, but I knew it wasn't good news.

My former fiancé returned holding a piece of paper. He looked as sorrowful as if his best friend had died. "Okay, Claire. What were you and Paul Morley arguing about?"

I heard a loud buzzing noise, but it was only in my head. Over the hum, I heard Abby's insinuation. "You were jealous." She went for the jugular. "You couldn't stand the thought he may have other women in his life."

"No. That's not true! As I said, we only went out a few times. Why would I even think we were exclusive?" This couldn't be happening. I was one of the good guys. I felt as if my stomach was being turned inside out.

Abby leaned over, palms flat on the table. "Why else would you have killed him?"

Corrigan's voice was calm, coaxing. "Was it self-defense, Claire?"

"I didn't kill him. I'm the one who got cut! I had to get stitches." I held up my arm. "See? I went to one of those urgent care places. Dr. Romansky. You can talk to him. And I have a receipt." The adrenaline my protest produced drained quickly when I realized the receipt I was about to wave under Abby's nose was somewhere in my living room. I mumbled, "I left the receipt at home. I called Paul to tell him how much it cost, but he didn't answer. I didn't know he was dead."

Hope flashed across Corrigan's face and then vanished so quickly I almost believed I imagined it. But Abby snorted, "Sure you did. So, what was the name of the clinic and what time were you there?"

My mind blanked. "It was probably about one in the afternoon, but I don't remember the name of the clinic. Just the doctor's name." I know none of that sounded reliable.

Corrigan's voice was level. "You know we'll find the receipt and check it against the time of death."

Abby's attention was on me like a shark's on its prey. "We'll find out the truth. We're going to find out that when Morley put up a fight, you got injured. And so you killed him."

It was suddenly too hot in the room and my palms felt moist. "I swear that's not what happened." I paused. "I want a lawyer."

Someone, I don't remember who, read me my rights and told me I was entitled to an attorney of my choice. Or one would be appointed.

℘ℛ

"GOLDFARB AND ASSOCIATES. How may I help you?" The woman's smooth voice did nothing to calm my nerves.

"Harold Goldfarb, please. This is Claire DeNardo calling." I tapped my foot and hoped Harold would take my call. The last time we saw each other we didn't part on happy terms. But he was the only lawyer I believed was wily enough to help me.

"I didn't think I'd be hearing from you any time soon, Claire." Usually, his very not-reached-puberty-yet voice irritated me, but at that moment it sounded like light at the end of the tunnel. "Not that your call isn't welcome."

Wishing that the uniformed officer watching me wouldn't pay such close attention, I whispered, "Harold, listen. I need your help. I've been charged with murder."

"I'm all ears." He actually sounded excited.

I pressed my lips together hard, then slowly, with great control, asked, "Have you heard about Paul Morley?"

"The attorney who was stabbed? Yes! Many of his colleagues, not me of course, are probably celebrating. And scrambling to get the poor man's clients." A beat. "You're telling me you're the POI they're questioning?"

Harold was undoubtedly rubbing his teensy hands together anticipating the exposure he'd get as my lawyer. "Yes, I'm that person of interest. Apparently I was the last one to see him alive, except for his real killer. Will you take my case?"

He cleared his throat, probably to tamp the thrill he was no doubt feeling. "I'll drop everything and be there immediately. Never fear, Claire. Justice will prevail."

The cop watching me leaned in. "Hey, I haven't got all day. Wrap it up."

I gave Harold my father's phone number and asked him to call my dad. After Harold promised he would, I ended the conversation. I'd be a model prisoner, but hopefully not a long term one.

Ushered back to my holding cell, I paced and waited for what seemed like hours.

A burly guard came up to the cell. "Ya got a visitor,

DeNardo."

The door opened and Harold Goldfarb strode in. I'd never been so happy to see any man in my whole life.

Naively, I believed Harold would be able to work some magic and convince Corrigan and Abby that I had nothing to do with Paul's death. But, after I poured out my story and answered his questions, he looked a bit concerned and I started to feel a lot less confident.

So much so, that by the time Harold and I reentered the interrogation room, my hopes of being released had nearly vanished. One glance at Abby and Corrigan, who were waiting to continue questioning me, and I knew my being released was a pipe dream.

Harold immediately laid the groundwork. "I'm sure, as seasoned detectives, you know this, but for formality sake, I'll remind you. All questions for my client will be directed to me."

"Yeah. Sure." Corrigan rubbed his chin. "Okay, Claire. Let's go over what you were doing at Paul Morley's boat."

I sighed and glanced at Harold. Once he gave me the nod, I began. Again. "We were supposed to go sailing, but the boat rocked and I fell into the knife he was holding." I took a breath and was about to continue, when Abby interrupted.

Claws drawn, she threatened me with, "A witness at the restaurant claims Morley was upset. That he hustled you out of the restaurant. You were mad, and when he tried to calm you down with a drink, you got even angrier.

What did he say that pushed you over the edge? That made you grab the knife and stab him? Tell us, Claire."

I dug my fingernails into the table. "No! We didn't argue! I wasn't mad. He was angry over a phone call he'd gotten. And whoever it was kept calling."

Abby practically hissed. "So, he was spending more time on the phone than with you. That made you mad. You wanted him to pay attention only to you. It's already pretty clear you get possessive."

Corrigan's eyes narrowed. "I don't think that's it." He stepped closer to me and coaxed. "Did you feel threatened by Morley? Did he come after you with the knife?"

"No. We were going to have Champagne. The boat rocked and I fell into the knife."

Abby sneered. "Then how did that knife end up in the victim's chest?"

Harold placed his hand on my forearm and spoke for me. "My client has already stated she'd fallen into the victim. Her prints could've easily gotten on the knife that way."

Abby continued to drill me as if Harold hadn't said a word. "You must've been furious with Morley." She muttered. "Besides, nobody opens a bottle of Champagne with a knife."

"Well, your victim did. Again, my client insists they weren't arguing." Harold sat back, arms folded.

The interview continued with other questions, but Abby kept returning to her Claire-stabbing-Morley-during-a-fight theory.

My wounded arm ached, and I clutched it to my chest.

In a paternal gesture, Harold placed his hand on my shoulder. "Detectives, surely you can see my client needs medical attention."

Corrigan leaned closer. "Claire, do you need a doctor right now?"

I gave no more than a slight shake of my head and Abby jumped right in again. "She'll get all the medical attention she needs, as soon as she tells us the truth about Paul Morley's death."

Harold's voice was as mellow as a yoga instructor's. "She's told you the truth and now, your fishing expedition is done, Officers."

An instant later, the detectives were called out of the room. I allowed myself a hopeful thought they'd let me go. But when they came back, Abby, with a glint in her eye, announced that I was under arrest for the murder of Paul Morley.

A uniformed officer slapped the handcuffs on me and led me from the interrogation room. I blinked back the tears forming in my eyes. They'd probably think they were tears of guilt. I felt as if I was standing on quicksand.

Harold spotted the tears and whispered, "Don't worry, Claire. You'll be out of here soon. In the meantime, I called your father. He'll take care of your dog."

Though thankful that Charlie would be okay, at that moment, my worry about spending my life in prison for a crime I didn't commit was foremost in my head.

Chapter Three

I WAS ON MY WAY to the Cuyahoga County Jail for processing. I told myself it wouldn't be so bad. I was wrong. This nightmare quickly got worse. I had to undress and be intimately inspected.

One of the guards then handed me an outfit that didn't exactly complement my dark hair and eyes. Plus, they hadn't shopped in the petite section. My feet vanished under the excess material though I'd pulled the pants up to my midriff. The top wasn't much better, but then I figured I wasn't here to win a Miss Criminality Beauty contest. I just needed to stay safe and alive until Harold could get me released.

A female cop who looked like she was made of bricks, ordered me to pick up the patched, scratchy blanket, threadbare sheet, and pillow that were assigned to me. After a quick stop at the infirmary for another dose of an antibiotic, the cop led me through a corridor, finally stopping at the fifth cell down. She sneered, "Time to meet your new friends." With that she shoved me and I stumbled into the cramped, dank room. She left then, abandoning me to the three inmates who already called this hole-in-the-wall home.

They stared at me, and I felt as vulnerable as a turtle without its shell. I forced myself to give a friendly, "I'm Claire."

The cellmate closest to me mumbled, "Your bunk's over there." She jutted her scarred double chin toward an upper bunk with a mattress so thin I was sure I'd be able to see through it.

Another woman was sitting on the bed below what was now my cot. She grinned, showing a missing tooth. "I'm Monique, your bunkmate." She nodded at the other two women. "The classy one there is Nadia. The other is Patch, because she's been patched up so many times." Monique's grin turned to a snarl. "Just remember, you're lowest on the totem pole here. What we say goes. You don't want nothing to happen to that cute face of yours."

She continued watching me like a vulture watching its trapped prey. I bobbed my head up and down. "Understood."

Patch eyed me as if I was a sirloin steak. "Hey. You got any food on you?"

Nadia chimed in with an enthusiastic, "Yeah! You got any?"

I shook my head, hoping I wouldn't get stabbed. "No. Sorry."

Nadia hopped off her cot and rubbed her flat belly. "Too bad. I'm hungry!"

Monique snorted. "Damn, Nadia! I don't know how you stay skinny. You eat like a teenage boy." She snorted, "Least with Patch, you can tell by her hips how much she likes to eat."

Relieved to have the attention taken off me for a moment, I grabbed a beaten-up step ladder, hoisted myself up and landed rear end first, on my mattress. Lumpy and stained, it was so thin I felt the metal slab on which it rested.

Thankfully, it was soon lights out and I wouldn't be forced to interact with these women. At least not until the next day.

In the dark, I curled into a ball, hoping to avoid the largest discolored spot on the mattress. I swallowed hard to stop from screaming. I tried telling myself this was no different than the time my parents forced me to go to summer camp. Bugs and bullies. Yeah. Sure. Except the bugs here were giant roaches and the bullies carried shivs.

।।।

BETWEEN AVOIDING THE lumps and stains of the mattress and listening to Patch's chain-saw snores, I hardly slept that night. Still, when the guard roused us the next morning for breakfast, I blinked a couple of times before the leaden feeling of hopelessness weighed me back down.

I followed my shuffling cellmates over to what was euphemistically called the cafeteria. The aroma of whatever was cooking did nothing to stimulate my appetite. The only good thing about this morning was that the ache in my arm was down to a dull throb.

Carrying my food tray, I glanced around the huge room and wondered where it'd be safest to sit. Nadia waved me over. Feeling as if I had no choice, I lowered myself onto the bench across from her and tried to scoop the thick beige slop from my bowl onto my plastic spoon.

Nadia tsk'd, "Don't bother with that." She grabbed my dish and turned it upside down. The pasty warm cereal didn't move. "Try the toast. It's the only thing edible." She glanced around at the other women. "Assuming you've got teeth." She shifted gears immediately. "So, what're you in for?"

"Murder."

She raised her perfectly shaped eyebrows. "You're kidding. Who? Boyfriend? Husband?"

"An attorney. But I didn't do it."

She chortled. "Yeah, all of us are innocent." She took a big gulp of water. "Personally, I think all the lawyers should be killed, and they can start with mine." A pause. "I used to work for a wealth management advisor you know, a financial planner. The company advised some bigwigs. But my boss got greedy, and I got blamed." Hey, mind if I eat your fruit cup?" She snatched it and ripped open the lid before I could respond. Spooning some in her mouth, she mumbled, "I guess not."

That left me the cold toast. Luckily, I wasn't really hungry anymore.

I was stacking my tray on the other used ones when I was ordered to the dispensary. They gave me another antibiotic for my arm wound and told me I had to come back later that day for the next dose and to have the wound's dressing changed. Guess they figured I didn't need any pain medication. Probably just as well. I had to keep my wits about me.

Walking back, the same guard who'd pushed me into my cell the day before told me my lawyer would see me that afternoon. I hoped with all my being Harold had some good news.

Rather than trying to bond with my cellmates, I kept to myself until it was time to meet with Harold.

When that moment came, I was led into a poorly lit room with grey walls that needed repainting.

Harold greeted me as if he was at my deathbed. With a hangdog look he murmured, "The Grand Jury will meet tomorrow to decide if they have enough to charge you. I'm very sorry this is happening this way."

I lost my patience and slapped the table. "Of course it shouldn't have happened this way. Now, find a way to make it unhappen!" Taking a deep breath, I regained control of myself. "Please, Harold."

He sat ramrod straight. "I'll do my absolute best."

His even more disheartening news was that the waitress who served Paul and me claimed we'd been arguing at the restaurant and the maître d' swore I was covered in blood when I left Paul's boat. *Great.* I was also the last person to see Paul alive. Things looked bad for me.

Harold folded his hands together. "What could be most damaging is that, as you know, your prints are on the murder weapon. I can't lie. The prosecution has a strong case."

It was as if someone had slipped a noose around my neck. It was so hard to breath. Finally, I cried, "I'm innocent."

"Of course you are, my dear. I wouldn't have taken this case otherwise."

Sure, but the publicity wouldn't hurt his career, either.

Harold's expression shifted, and he looked more confident than he had a minute ago. "There's a question of time of death versus when that maître d' spotted you. The police think it's close enough. I believe I can stretch," he motioned as if pulling taffy, "the discrepancy out to make it questionable that you could have killed him."

That gave me a smidgen of hope. I struggled to take a deep breath and regained some composure. "The morning he died, Paul was talking to someone on the phone and it was nasty. The person kept calling. Remember? I told you about it. Have you found out who that was? Maybe somehow they killed Paul."

Harold reviewed his notes. "I've requested the victim's phone records. I'm hoping to get them today." Harold paused and then he flipped to another page. "I've also been looking into cases Morley handled recently. It could be a disgruntled client was calling him."

Our time was almost up. I leaned over the table. "Harold, please. I'm counting on you!"

He almost saluted me. "Never fear, Claire."

The rest of Sunday passed achingly slowly. Lunch was as dismal as breakfast. By dinner, I was famished. Nadia again insisted I sit with her. Probably so she could eat off my tray again. That was impossible though, because by that last meal of the day, I chowed down on every last unidentifiable morsel.

Nadia sniggered, "Hey, I guess you're like the rest of us. Get hungry enough and you'll even eat this slop."

Spitting out a piece of gristle, I nodded. "And I am hungry enough." How I wished for a piece of my aunt's triple chocolate layer cake! To take my mind off what I may never have again, I asked, "So, you're in for robbery?"

"Embezzlement. At least that's what they're trying to prove. My arraignment is stalled. It's finally tomorrow. I was the bookkeeper at Pilkosky and Hunt. I swear, though, if I ever get out of here, I'll prove that Ben Pilkosky framed me."

"Can't your lawyer help?"

She practically spit. "If he could, I wouldn't be sitting here with you." Out of the side of her mouth she asked, "So what'd you do before you arrived here?"

I bit my lower lip and debated whether to tell her the truth. "Well, I was, am a sort of—"

Misinterpreting my hesitation, she whispered, "You're a cop!" When I shook my head, she sneered. "A lawyer?"

"Private investigator."

"Really?" She ran her fingers through her cropped platinum blonde hair. "You think you could help me?"

"How? I can't even help myself."

Her grayish cat-like eyes shifted from side to side, as if checking to make sure nobody was listening. She leaned over so far, I could smell her not-so-fresh breath. "Get some proof I didn't take any of that money. Help me and maybe I can help you."

The loud din in the room faded in my ears. "How?"

She gave me a mysterious smile. "Do it and you'll see."

I wanted to grab her wrist and demand that she tell me now, but a guard approached me. "Hey, DeNardo, somebody wants to talk to you."

Probably not good news. "Who?"

The guard's upper lip curled. "Prisoners don't ask questions."

Nadia muttered, "I'll take care of your tray."

I didn't move from the bench, the fatty, tasteless meat I'd just ingested tried to work its way back up into my throat.

"Come on, DeNardo! I don't have all day!" The guard grabbed my arm and pulled me from my seat. She led me down a corridor to one of the meeting rooms, and then opened the door. "Go on in."

The light was rather dim and I blinked twice, surprised at who I saw.

Corrigan.

The shock on my face clued him on the need for an explanation. He cleared his throat. "Probably wondering why I'm here."

Even if I had a snappy comeback, I didn't dare use it. He was now on the *other side*. I nodded.

"Have a seat." He motioned to one of the chairs at a small table, but he remained standing. Once I sat down, he began. "I shouldn't even be here, but I need to know. How important to you was Morley?"

I blinked hard. *He came all this way to ask me that?* I tried to keep my anger and sense of betrayal buried, but they crawled out. "I told you at the police station. The guy was actually a jerk. This was going to be our last date!"

He stopped pacing and leaned over the table. "You may not believe this, but I'm trying to help you."

I could smell his cologne and a wave akin to homesickness washed over me, but I steeled myself. Maybe this was a trick. "Isn't it a little late for that? It would've been nice if you'd done it before I landed here."

He slapped the table and I jumped. "Dammit, Claire. I wanted to back then, but the evidence…Look, I'm willing to do some digging to see if we've missed anything. On my own time."

A teensy spark of hope flickered, but I couldn't afford to fan it. "Why would you do that?"

His face softened. "You have to ask?"

I crossed my arms. "Yes, I do."

He plopped into the chair across from me. "I know you well enough to know you're not a cold-blooded killer."

Not exactly a declaration of any remaining feelings for me, but I'd take it. "You're right. I'm not. But before I say anything, swear to me this isn't a trick."

He made an X across his heart. "I swear. Now, tell me everything that happened that day."

I repeated everything I knew. Maybe by repeating it, some forgotten detail would pop up. It didn't, but I let that flicker of hope grow and it warmed me all the way back to my cell.

Chapter Four

AUNT LENA, Ed, my father and his wife, Suzy, sat at the back of the courtroom where I was being arraigned. My aunt sadly waved to me, tissue in hand, as if I were being sent to a gulag in Siberia.

I tried to smile at my family, but I doubt it was very convincing. I wanted to talk to them, assure them, but the judge entered the courtroom before I could.

Harold tapped my arm to get my attention when my name was called. Standing to face the judge, my legs felt as if they'd give out under me.

The fiftyish-looking judge, almost drowning in her black robe, wearily addressed me. "You're being charged with murder in the second degree." Quickly, as if she'd done this a million times, she asked me how I pled.

In that moment my aunt yelled, "She's innocent! Anyone with half a brain knows that!" I squeezed my eyes shut. Thanks to Aunt Lena, I'd probably be sent to Sing-

Sing for the rest of my life.

The judge lowered her eyebrows and pointed her gavel toward my aunt. "Another outbreak and you'll be held in contempt. Understood?"

She returned her eagle stare to me. "Regardless of your cheering section, what do you plead?"

I held my head high and hoped I looked innocent. "Not guilty, Your Honor."

The question of bail then came up. The prosecuting attorney argued that I'd committed a savage attack and shouldn't be out on bail. Harold, in his element now, puffed out his chest, ready for battle. "Your Honor, how could this petite young woman have so brutally stabbed the victim, who we all know was a husky man?"

"Save it for the jury, Mr. Goldfarb." The judge upheld my original bail. I could be released for $500,000. She might as well have set it at five million.

Harold handed me a note my father had just given him. It said that my dad would take care of the bail and not to worry. I'd be out before I knew it. I looked at my father to acknowledge his message. The lines on his face told me he'd be worrying enough for the both of us.

Despite my doubts, my dad was as good as his word and my bail was posted an hour later.

My aunt and Suzy left earlier together and Ed and my father took me home. My dad spoke first. "Suzy's been taking care of Charlie, but I'll bet he misses you."

I gave him a big hug, hoping that would convey all my gratitude and remorse for the pain I must have been causing him. "Thank you, Dad. Tell Suzy I appreciate it so much."

"Will do." He faux-grumbled, "Ya know, she thinks Charlie's so cute, now she's talking about getting a mutt too."

I knew my dad was trying to keep it light, but with trepidation I asked, "How did you raise the money for my bail?"

Ed spoke up. "Now don't you give that any thought."

That's when I knew. "Aunt Lena. Did she use *Cannoli's* as collateral for the bondsman?" If my mood was a color, it would have turned from blue to black. "Please say she didn't!"

Ed held up his hand. "You're my boss, but I gotta tell you. Now's not the time to worry about that. Our first priority is to find out who really offed that lawyer."

My shoulders slumped and I felt as if I were carrying the weight of all my failures. Still, I managed a half-hearted, "You're right." Still, I wanted to weep. *My aunt's livelihood, her future, all at risk because of me.*

Even once we pulled into *Cannoli's* parking lot, I sat there, staring down at my hands.

My dad got out and opened my door. "Come on, pumpkin. Your aunt and everyone else is waiting inside to see you."

I dragged myself out of the car, walking so slowly, my dad got ahead of me. He opened the door to the bakery, and Aunt Lena rushed toward me. She threw her beefy arms around me and drew me close. As always, she smelled of vanilla, and I inhaled deeply, as if I'd recently been deprived of air.

Behind Aunt Lena was her best friend and longtime assistant, Angie, who was wearing a smile as big as a quarter of a cantaloupe. Her son, David, my ex-infatuation and now friend, stood next to her.

He put his hands on both my shoulders. "Claire, really glad to see you."

"Thanks, David. And thank you. All of you." With all this attention and love, my eyes misted and my voice broke.

Aunt Lena cleared her throat. "Hey, no time for tears. I baked that chocolate cake you like so much. Come on back with me. You get the first piece." She grabbed me by the arm and practically dragged me into the kitchen.

While she was cutting me a huge piece of the dessert my taste buds most desired, the rest of me was committed to letting my aunt know how grateful I was for her help. "Aunt Lena, I don't know how to thank you—"

"That's right. You don't know how. But I do. You find the so-and-so who really killed that lawyer and clear your name. Now eat." She shoved a fork in my hand and waved the plated cake under my nose.

I was a goner. The cake was like silk on my tongue. The chocolate frosting should have been declared one of the great wonders of the world. For one moment I forgot all about my troubles. "Aunt Lena, this cake is wonderful. I love you and I swear you and my dad will get back every penny you put towards my bail."

Aunt Lena didn't even have a chance to respond because Ed came into the kitchen with my phone.

"Kiddo, hate to break up this soiree, but your lawyer called twice while you were in here. Must be important."

My throat tightened and suddenly the cake's sweet aroma nauseated me. "Sorry, but I better take this." I took the phone from Ed's hand and stepped outside to return Harold's call.

My lawyer didn't waste time with any pleasantries. "I have Morley's phone records."

My heart jumped in my chest. "And?"

He blew out a deep breath. "Two of the calls Morley received the day he died were from a fellow named Tommy Allegro. Are you acquainted with him?"

"No. Should I be?"

"He's allegedly done some work for a gentleman you do know. Michael Bucanetti."

Until that moment, I doubted anything could dismay or surprise me about Paul Morley's murder. But the mention of big time Pittsburgh mobster now living in Cleveland, Michael Bucanetti, made me feel as if my nerves had been lit on fire. He and I had tangled during previous cases and the man was, quite frankly, terrifying. Thankfully, we had called a truce, and that's the way I wanted to keep it. But Ed was looking at me expectantly and Harold waited on the other end of the phone. I bit my lower lip. "So, what's next?" Though I knew *next* was going to be on me.

Harold cleared his throat. "As you will no doubt recall,

I've had some dealings with Mr. Bucanetti, but not with Tommy Allegro." He stopped, probably hoping I'd volunteer my PI staff of one to investigate. "I know you'd like to keep my billable hours down, so…"

My insides tightened, but I felt I had no choice. As long as I remained in jail, my accounts receivable would stay at zero. "Good point." I took a deep breath to fortify myself. "My colleagues and I will delve into Allegro's business with Paul."

The celebration for my freedom was over pretty quickly after that. I thanked everyone again and then asked my father if he'd drive me home first to say hello to Charlie and take him for a walk. Then Ed and I would meet up at my office after he did some digging into Tommy Allegro's interests.

This was one case that had to be solved as quickly as possible. Returning to that jail cell would be unbearable. Despite it being cool outside, my hands felt clammy and I could almost detect the less-than-pleasing smell of women inside those close quarters.

Chapter Five

DAD DROPPED ME off at home, and I hurried to my apartment door. I could hear Charlie's excited whimpers and scratches on the other side. I turned the key and Charlie rushed at me, dancing on his two back legs as he pawed at me with his front ones. I hugged him and whispered how much I'd missed him.

I grabbed his leash, and we headed outside for a quick excursion. Then we returned to the apartment. I changed out of my arraignment clothes and into a more comfortable outfit. Charlie followed me around as if he were tethered to me.

Finally ready, I squatted down to Charlie's level. "I'm leaving now, but I'll be back real soon." Despite that promise, my precious dog looked at me so pitifully, I relented. After all, it was DeNardo and Son, and since Charlie was the son, he had a right to come to work every so often.

My comment, "Okay, Charlie. You can come too." Was greeted with yips and running in a circle.

We'd reached my office building's parking lot when my phone rang. It was Harold. "I believe I have the person who can help you get better acquainted with Mr. Allegro and his, um, enterprises. Her name is Iris. She's his former wife and I'm sure, a wealth of information."

I blew a breath into my bangs. "Thank you, Harold. I've just gotten to the office. Can you text me her information?" Charlie picked that moment to bark.

"I didn't realize you worked in a kennel." He chuckled at his own joke. "Of course, I'll send it over. And consider this a freebie." With that he ended the call and it wasn't long until I had his text.

It felt strange entering my office, as if I'd been gone years instead of a few days. Charlie quickly distracted me by heading into the kitchen, no doubt sniffing a stale donut. I pulled on his leash. "You're staying with me."

I was surprised that Ed hadn't made it back to my office, but rather than sit around waiting, I powered up my computer to see what else I could find on Iris. The more information I had on her, the better prepared I would be. I had already had enough unwanted surprises and I didn't want more.

It couldn't have been more than ten minutes later when Charlie, who had decided to rest by my desk, perked up and growled softly, putting me on edge. I'd had unwelcome visitors before but being out on bail, I couldn't carry a gun. I picked up my stapler, as if I could stop a possible assailant by stapling his head to the doorframe. I waited.

A sultry perfume preceded the woman who entered my office. With her bright red lipstick, bleached blonde bob, and fur jacket even in May, she reminded me of a gun moll from one of the black-and-white mysteries I'd watched with my dad. Maybe the Maltese Falcon. Except I wasn't Humphrey Bogart.

She held out a manicured hand with nails that matched her lipstick. "I'm Iris. Thank God, the *former,* Mrs. Tommy Allegro."

It took me a moment to find my voice. "Thank you for coming in."

Charlie, ever my defender, lowered his head to be petted.

Iris scratched behind my dog's ear and her bracelets jangled. "Hey, no prob. That funny little guy, Harold, asked me to come in." She pursed her lips as if sucking a lemon. "Then he asked me to dinner, but I don't go out with guys the same height as me."

I suppressed a grin. "Please, have a seat."

"Sure, thanks." Her skin-tight skirt made it difficult for her to gracefully lower herself into the chair, but when she finally landed she said, "I want to make something clear. I didn't know a thing about what Tommy was into until way after we got hitched."

"Understood. Now, could you tell me exactly what you didn't know about?"

She swallowed hard and ran her hand down her neck.

"First, you got anything to drink? I'm as dry as that plant you got dying over there." She pointed to the wilted philodendron behind my desk.

"I can make some coffee or tea. Or would water do?"

She heaved a dissatisfied sigh. "You don't got anything stronger?"

"Well, I have some leftover Prosecco. It's probably flat but you're welcome to it."

She shrugged. "I'll give it a try."

I brought her a glass of the no longer sparkling wine. Without a pause, she downed it. "Okay. Now I can talk."

She snarled. "You should know that Tommy cheated me out of the alimony I deserve. So now, I want that SOB to burn in Hell. But first he should spend the rest of his rotten life in prison."

So much for my wondering why she was so willing to talk to me. But before we continued, I asked, "Have you spoken to the police about your ex-husband's activities?"

She shrunk back as if I'd thrown hot coffee at her. "No. The cops and me don't exactly see eye to eye." She smoothed the fur on her jacket. "What with my former occupation, the less I talk to them, the better, you know?"

"All right." With her flashy appearance, I could only imagine what she used to do for a living. "So, let's go back. What didn't you know about Tommy?"

She glanced around nervously, as if expecting her ex-husband to leap out of a closet. "He's cozy with a lot of loan sharks. He may even be one. Anyway, lots of money passes through him. And it ain't all his. If you know what

I mean."

The hairs on my neck stood up. Could Paul have owed Tommy money? Money he couldn't pay back?

"Okay." I said, "Tommy knows a lot of shady people. But what do you know about his relationship with an attorney named Paul Morley?"

She nodded, knowingly. "Yeah, the lawyer who got killed. Him and Tommy were tight. Least for a while. They'd meet downtown at the Chophouse and have drinks. Maybe dinner." She pouted. "I only got invited once and that was before me and Tommy got married."

"Do you remember anything they talked about?"

She shrugged. "Sports. Who made the best martinis. That kinda stuff."

My shoulders dropped. "That's it?"

"Well, that one time I got to go with Tommy, about halfway through dinner, I went to the little girls' room. When I came back, Tommy and that guy were hunched close to each other, like they were talking about something serious. Maybe even illegal. I couldn't help myself, and I asked about it." She wrinkled her nose. "You'da thought I asked what kind of underwear their mothers wore. They clammed up. Never got invited again."

I blew out a deep, disappointed breath. "Is there anything else you can tell me? Any information could be helpful."

"Just this." She pulled something from her purse. "A few months before we split, Tommy was sneaking around at night. I figured there was another woman, so I went through his stuff. This is all I found. Here." She handed me an embossed card that read Pilkosky and Hunt. The person's name on the card was Benjamin Pilkosky. I recalled my conversation with fellow prisoner, Nadia. She'd worked for that same firm and claimed she'd been framed.

I struggled to keep my voice calm. "Did you ever ask him about his connection to Benjamin Pilkosky?"

"Nah. Didn't want to risk him knowing I was checking up on him. Just kept the card in case. You know." She wiped her mouth with the back of her hand. "I'm getting kinda dry again. You wanna talk more about this over a drink?"

It was plain that Iris was wrangling for more liquid refreshment. I couldn't go with her, but she'd definitely given me some useful information. "I don't think I can join you, but at least let me buy you a drink." I handed her a well-worn ten-dollar bill. "Well, thank you very much for coming in." I stood and extended my hand. "Please, if you think of anything else, let me know."

She rose and grasped my offered hand. "Sure. I'd love to see that snake in a prison uniform."

I escorted her through the door into the hallway and watched as she sashayed toward the stairs, almost bumping into Ed, who was hurrying to my office. A friendly, quick exchange passed between the two of them.

Reaching me he wiped his forehead. "Whew! Was that shapely creature Iris?"

I tsk'd and shook my head. "Come on. We've got to

take Charlie home. I'll fill you in on the way."

After we dropped my upset pup off, Ed, ankle resting on his opposite thigh, listened carefully to what Iris had told me. "Sounds like there's more to the goings on between Morley and Tommy Allegro than just an appreciation for a good drink. I also bet it's no coincidence Tommy knows Pilkosky. All that money changing hands and nobody looking too close." He shook his head and uncrossed his legs. "I talked to a guy who knew Tommy Allegro from way back when. Seems Allegro liked his dough clean."

"Clean money?" My jaw dropped as the light came on in my head. "Money laundering?"

"Scrubbed and hung up to dry. 'Cept Allegro never got caught, and for at least the last five years has claimed to be legit. Owns seven bowling alleys in Ohio." He snorted. "Now they call 'em entertainment centers. Ya know, bowling plus laser tag, plus video games, and a bar and grill."

I'd seen the places Ed was talking about. "Fun Times? Those are his places?" I was wondering if I needed to brush up on my bowling skills when Ed leaned over my desk.

"So, what do we do with this information? Work it ourselves? Or, bring it to Brian?"

Unsure whether Corrigan would even want my information, I clasped and unclasped my hands. "I'd rather work it myself, but given my circumstances, maybe giving it to Corrigan is the wiser choice."

Ed's firm nod told me he heartily agreed.

I was taken aback when Corrigan answered his phone, and I stammered, "Uh, hi, Brian. I uh…I think we have a lead on someone who may have had a reason to kill Paul Morley."

"Okay, Claire. I'm listening."

I took a deep breath, collecting my thoughts. "Have you heard of Tommy Allegro?" Before he could even answer, I continued. "He's a suspected money launderer, a probable associate of Michael Bucanetti *and* he called Paul twice the day Paul was murdered." With my next breath, I was prepared to tell him about Benjamin Pilkosky but my thoughts were drowned by the volume of Corrigan's carrying-the-weight-of-the-world sigh.

"We're well aware of Tommy Allegro and that he called Morley. I've already questioned him and he's got an alibi."

My twinkle of hope dimmed, but didn't die. "Maybe his alibi isn't airtight. Or he hired someone to commit the murder."

"Even if his alibi was shaky, which it isn't, I'd need more than just phone calls. Like motive."

"Well, maybe if somebody looked harder, they'd find a motive." I winced. *Sarcasm? Really, Claire?*

Luckily, Corrigan didn't rise to my baiting. Instead, he turned it on me. "Claire, that somebody better not be you. While you're out on bail, you can't associate with known criminals. Understood?"

"Yes, sir." I felt like a child being reprimanded by the

school principal, and I didn't like it.

Unexpectedly, he softened his tone. "Look, whatever's gone on between us, I still want you safe and out of jail. I'm doing everything I can to make that happen. Give me the chance. Okay?"

My indignation melted, "Yeah, okay." I hoped he wouldn't go further and ask me to swear that I wouldn't do my own investigating. That was a promise I wouldn't be able to keep.

"Great. I'm going through everything twice, three times. I'll find out who the real killer is, Claire."

Relief I hadn't expected to feel washed over me. "Thank you, Brian. I do appreciate it. Now, there's something else you should know—"

A yell so loud I heard it through the phone stopped me. Corrigan whispered, "Captain wants me now. I've gotta go." He ended the call.

I glared at my phone as if it was responsible for my not getting to tell Corrigan about Pilkosky and his possible tie-in. Deciding to turn my frustration toward some useful action, I addressed Ed. "Okay, the police aren't going to do anything with this information. It's up to us."

Ed looked doubtful. "Aren't you forgetting that you just got out on bail?"

Through gritted teeth I replied, "I don't need you to remind me." I took a deep breath. "Sorry. Look, I know I'm taking a big risk by going after the real killer. Yeah, I'll end up back in jail, but if I don't do something, I could be spending the rest of my life there."

"I gotcha. So, what's the plan, boss?"

"How does going bowling sound?"

Chapter Six

AS IT TURNED OUT, we didn't need to actually go bowling. The corporate headquarters for Fun Times was above their flagship operation in the Flats, an area primarily devoted to restaurants, bars, and the like.

Halfway there, Ed shifted in his passenger seat. "Tell me again what you're hoping to get from talking to Allegro? We'd be better off doing our snooping after hours, if you get my drift."

I didn't answer right away, because, truthfully, I wasn't sure. I pushed down on the gas pedal and stared ahead. "I have to do *something*, and right now I can't risk being caught entering anyplace illegally. So, we'll try the nice way first."

"You're the boss." He didn't exactly sound on board. "But let me go on record as saying I think this visit could blow up in our faces. And that's the best scenario."

I bit my lower lip and prayed silently this wasn't going

to be a fiasco or worse.

Ed and I entered the entertainment center and were immediately dazed by the noise and blinking lights. This place could give somebody a migraine. A burly man in a black tee-shirt stood by an elevator down a corridor away from the festivities. "Ed," I whispered. "I'll bet you a chocolate martini that elevator will take us to Tommy Allegro's office."

Ed nodded and tilted his head toward the guy by the elevator. "Yeah, but first we'd have to get past King Kong there."

"I've got an idea. Stay here." I removed my jacket and unbuttoned the top two buttons on my shirt. Ignoring Ed's bemused look, I walked over to the man, swinging my hips as if I was trying to knock against each wall of the corridor. "Hey there!" I used what I hoped sounded like a flirty voice, "is Tommy upstairs? He promised to buy me a drink tonight."

The guy crossed his arms, revealing biceps the size of small mountains. "Who the hell are you?"

I swallowed my fear that he'd knock me across the floor and continued the charade. "Claire!"

He snarled, "Mr. Allegro didn't tell me about nobody coming. Now, get lost."

Giving it one more try I pouted as prettily as I could. "I bet Tommy will be mad he missed me."

I swear this gigantic man's eyes turned red. I thought he'd punch me with his anvil-like fists, but the elevator doors opened just then. A short, slender man stepped out.

He was well-dressed and well-groomed, with dark hair slicked back 1950's style, even though he looked to be only about forty. He wasn't ugly by any means, but he reminded me of a weasel with his narrow face that almost came to a point.

The big guy practically bowed to the weasel-man. "Good evening, Mr. Allegro."

"Mr. Allegro!" I skirted around the jumbo-sized guard. "I need to talk to you."

Mr. Massive guy's hand wrapped tightly around my arm and he yanked me away from Allegro. "You're outta here. I'm sorry, sir."

"Just a minute, Maurice." Tommy held up his hand. "Let's hear what she has to say." He glanced at Ed, who had stepped forward to no doubt rescue me from Maurice. Tommy's gaze returned to me, specifically, to my chest. It was as if I was a chicken and he was a ravenous fox. "Let's go to my office. Just the two of us."

I shot a look to Ed not to interfere. I could certainly handle the situation myself. Never mind that my heart was beating so hard I wondered if Tommy could see it throbbing against my chest. I glanced down, wishing I hadn't unbuttoned the top button on my blouse.

Allegro leered, "Honey, you don't need to worry. Tommy takes good care of people he likes."

Great. He refers to himself in the third person. Don't serial killers do that? Despite a bead of perspiration rolling down between my breasts, I smiled at him as best I could. "Mr. Allegro, I—"

"Call me Tommy."

"Tommy. I just have a couple of questions for you."

The door opened and he escorted me out of the elevator. "I know." His voice turned cold. "I also know who you are."

I stopped, and I believe my heart did too. "What?"

He smirked and his face became even more weasel-like. "Yeah, your face is all over the news. You're that DeNardo broad accused of knocking off Paul Morley." He dragged me into a spacious, well-appointed office. "Sit down."

Having no choice, I plopped into a plush chair, wondering how much damage I could inflict by swinging my purse at him.

He leaned against a stately mahogany desk and gave me a cocky smile. "Gotta say, pictures don't do you justice. If things were different, me and you could get real cozy."

I suppressed the urge to grimace at the thought.

His smile disappeared. "Now, I brought you up here for a reason."

I scrunched into the chair wishing I could disappear into it.

His upper lip curled. "Hey, you don't need to look like I'm gonna eat ya or nothing. I just wanna tell you, I'm not who you're looking for."

"How do you," I cleared my throat so that my words could actually be heard. "Know who I'm looking for?"

"Lady, everyone who's anyone on the street knows

you're trying to find someone to take the rap you went to jail for. And I ain't it." He ran his tongue around his mouth. "But, I'll give you a hint."

I realized he wasn't going to maim me and blew out a shaky breath. "Why do you want to help me?"

"Ain't a question of *wanting* to help. You and that detective are stinking up the atmosphere with your questions. Cops snooping around is never good for business. So, I help you, you help me by steering the police, especially that hot-shot detective, Corrigan, away from me. Deal?"

I sat up straight and clasped my hands tightly so he couldn't see them trembling. "Before I agree, tell me why you called Paul that day."

He gave me a one-sided smile. "Well, sweetheart, that'll cost you one more button."

Fumbling with the next one down, I ridiculously felt relieved I'd worn a non-see-through padded bra.

His look was pure vulture. Then he shrugged. "Money was disappearing. Him and me needed to talk about where it went."

"Did he tell you?"

"One question and I answered it. Sorry, you don't get no more."

I could tell by his tone there was no bargaining. "Okay. You've got a deal" And I'd deal later with getting Corrigan off Tommy's scent.

He pressed his lips together and pointed his finger at me. "One more thing. You gotta keep your mouth shut about who gave you this information. Nobody I know rats on somebody and lives long." He rested his right hand under his suit jacket near his left shoulder, letting me know he had a gun resting in its holster. "Get my meaning?"

I made a motion as if zipping my lips. "Definitely. Not a word."

He nodded. "My take, is, if you wanna know where there was trouble, look into Morley's financial advisor and associates."

"Pilkosky and Hunt?"

"Even Morley's son thought there was something not right. But you never heard any of that from me. Now, unbutton your shirt."

I clutched my collar. "What? That isn't part of the deal!"

With a wave of his hand, he said, "Nah, this ain't what you think. I can't let you get outta here without it looking like I got my way. Just unbutton and then button up but wrong, ya know?"

Sometimes I'm slow, but this time I understood. "You mean that for anyone who might be interested in what was going on here, you want it to look like there's been no talk, just, um, action?"

"You got it. Now, hurry up with the blouse. I got places to be."

My fingers fumbled with the buttons as if I had popsicle sticks instead of fingers, making it slow going.

"Come on!" The moment I finished, he grabbed my arm and yanked me out of the chair, pulling me against him. He covered my mouth with his. I smelled his cologne and tobacco, and his heavy beard scratched my chin. I pushed him away and he wiped his mouth and laughed. "It looks more real now."

In the elevator, Tommy loosened his tie and pulled out his shirttails, so that by the time we reached the ground floor, it was easy to believe we'd had a very brief encounter.

The body guard took one look and nodded his approval.

Ed's eyes widened and then became pinpoints. His hands curled into fists.

To stop him from doing something we'd all regret, I rushed to him, grabbed him by the shoulders, and whispered, "It's not what you think."

I could feel Ed relax just a bit, and I let go.

Tommy smirked at Ed, "She's okay, old man. To tell ya the truth, though, I've had better."

Ed's eyes flashed, but he didn't make a move.

Tommy brushed past us, whistling.

Out of the corner of my mouth, I said, "Let's get out of here, Ed. I'll explain in the car."

Apparently, Ed couldn't wait that long. We'd barely reached the parking lot when he halted. "You better spill it now, before I have a stroke."

Nobody followed us outside, so I felt relatively safe. Still, I wanted to get to my car as quickly as possible. "Okay, I can talk while we walk." I filled Ed in on what Tommy had said, unhesitatingly omitting the physical parts.

Ed just listened until we got into the car. He then harrumphed, "When I took this job, I promised Lena I'd watch over you. Ya know, make sure you didn't do anything…against your best judgment." He nodded toward my chest. "But those buttons didn't get buttoned wrong by themselves. And that razor burn…"

I clasped my hands and came clean with the rest of the story.

Ed fumed. "Yeah, he wanted to make it real, all right. If he ever tries to get real again with you, just let me know." He made a fist. "And I'll make sure he gets *real* hurt."

I looked Ed in the eye. "I appreciate you wanting to protect my virtue. But I'm a big girl now and, honestly, I can take care of myself. Now, turn around so I can fix my blouse." Looking down at my buttons, I murmured, "We need to find who handled Paul's investments at Pilkosky and Hunt."

Glancing at his watch, Ed shook his head. "Can't do it tonight. Me and Lena signed up for *cumbia* lessons. First one's tonight." He swayed his upper body in time to an imaginary beat.

"That Columbian dance? Really?"

He winked. "Gets the blood boiling, ya know."

"No, and I don't want to know." I took a breath. "Okay, I'll dig on my own. But tomorrow, I want you to find out what you can about Paul Morley's son. I knew he had a boy and girl, but Paul gave me the impression they were just kids. Except children don't usually have opinions about financial dealings. At least none I've known."

Dropping Ed off at his car I walked back into my office, aiming to Google what I could about Paul's dealings with Pilkosky and Hunt. In so doing, I ran across a news story about that firm's scandal.

Good God! Nadia, my cellmate, was front and center as the alleged perpetrator of the stolen monies. I recalled how she'd complained to me that her former employer, Benjamin Pilkosky wealth management advisor, had framed her. But, in this story, Pilkosky was painted as much a victim as those clients who'd lost their life savings. My lips curled from the sour taste this story left.

If this was the way everyone was going to paint it, Nadia didn't stand a chance. I also remembered, though, how she'd strongly hinted she could help me if I helped her. At this point, I could use all the help I could get. Even if some of it was from a dubious source. No doubt Nadia was still in jail. I'll go visit her in the morning and if her story rang true, I'd see what I could do to get her out. I was lost in thought as to how I could accomplish that when my business phone rang. "DeNardo and Son. This is Claire. Can I help you?"

"They were right, then." It was a young woman.

"Excuse me? Right about what? Who is this?"

"Janette Morley. The daughter of the man you murdered."

Chapter Seven

I CLEARED MY throat, giving myself a chance to think. All I could come up with was, "I'm sorry for your loss, but I didn't kill your father."

She harrumphed. "I didn't call to argue with you." My mouth moved as I tried to form a question, but her next words stopped me cold. "I want you to find my brother, Dylan."

If I hadn't already been seated, I would have fallen into my chair. "Why would you want *me* to find him, assuming he's missing?"

"Actually, I don't really believe you killed my father. In fact, I'm sure you didn't."

My eyes popped wide open and I wondered if I was hearing right. "I'm glad you feel that way, but—"

"Meet me outside the Tango Room at nine tonight and I'll explain everything."

My confusion and disbelief gave way to curiosity. "How will I know it's you?"

Her voice was icy. "Picture my father with long hair." She ended the call.

I glanced at the time. It'd take me thirty minutes to get there, leaving me with another thirty minutes, enough time to search for information on both Dylan and Janette Morley.

I'd scarcely begun when my personal phone rang. Corrigan.

My mind was darting in different directions. Tell him about Tommy Allegro? Confess I agreed to meet with Janette Morley?

Say nothing. See what he wants.

These thoughts scattered with the hope the actual murderer was now in police custody. I struggled to steady my voice. "Hi, Brian. What's up?"

"I wanted to make sure you're okay."

I forced myself to keep calm but the sarcasm bled through. "Oh, I'm fine. Just fine. Why wouldn't I be?"

He sighed. "Yeah. I get it. I also called to update you."

My pulse sped up. Maybe he *had* found the real killer. Maybe then I wouldn't have to somehow pull him off Tommy Allegro's tail. "And?"

"I've been putting pressure on Tommy Allegro and his sleazebag operation." His frustration wove its way through words. "Not much success there. But you never know."

I felt as if I was stuck in mud. There was no way I could tell Corrigan about my meeting with Tommy. At least not without my life coming to a quick and nasty ending. Still, I needed Corrigan off that trail. I inhaled and went for it. "You know, there's a good chance it wasn't Tommy Allegro. I mean, Tommy may be a lot of things, but I don't believe he killed Paul." I rushed to add, "Have you by chance questioned Paul's son, Dylan?"

He blew out a breath. "We haven't been able to get hold of him. He's in Nepal for some spiritual thing. According to the airline's records, Dylan Morley left for Nepal a week before his father was killed. We've been trying to reach him through the embassy in China. You can imagine how that's going. Why?"

I recapped my conversation with Janette Morley leaving out, for the moment, my meeting with her. I didn't want him to show up and maybe spook her. "She suspects her brother because she claims he didn't want to wait for his inheritance."

He listened without stopping me. I could almost hear his brain spinning. "Maybe Janette Morley wants her brother as the killer so she doesn't have to share that inheritance. But wishing doesn't make it so." He paused, then conjectured, "Wouldn't be the first time siblings betrayed each other over money, though. Could even be that Janette's the real killer…"

I interrupted his thoughts. "Have you looked into Paul's financial advisors? Pilkosky and Hunt?"

Silence. Yet it seemed so loud and felt so heavy.

Not surprisingly, right then Corrigan did what he always did. He discounted what I'd brought to the table. Like a wounded tigress, I was ready to lash out, but I decided maybe it was best that he disagreed. I'd investigate both the wealth managers and Dylan myself.

That pumped me up, and I was ready to agree with him just to end the call.

But he shocked me. "On second thought, there may be something to the brother-sister-father relationship we missed the first time around. And it sure wouldn't hurt to look closer at Morley's money men." He cleared his throat. "I'll do that. You know, you've turned into a helluva good investigator."

My jaw could have hit my shins. *He never said that before.*

"Claire, I've gotta go now."

Before I could get my next thoughts organized, he ended the call.

I put my phone down as my spirits lifted. I was in a horrible situation; accused of a murder I didn't commit, and worried about my aunt losing her business because of my bail. Yet surprisingly, stupidly I felt lighter. Could Corrigan actually believe in me and my detective skills, just a bit?

I shook my head hard to knock that idea out, telling myself it didn't make any difference what he thought. It was too little, much too late. Water under the bridge. All that stuff. Yet, as I grabbed my purse to go meet with

Janette, the corners of my mouth turned up just a tiny bit.

In the time it took me to drive over to see Paul Morley's daughter, I'd banished Corrigan and his faint praise from my brain. I had more important matters to attend. Like finding out who killed Paul and thus exonerating myself.

The parking lot to the Tango Room was still fairly empty. Though it was early, I was a few minutes late and worried Paul's daughter wouldn't be there.

I released my breath when I spotted a young woman standing in the doorway outside the restaurant. Janette was right about one thing. She resembled how Paul must have looked in his youth. The exception being, she had long, ash-blond hair, as opposed to Paul's dark brown.

Parking my car, I hustled toward her. "Janette?"

She nodded. "I didn't go inside yet. They serve booze and I wasn't sure you could. Being out on bail and all…" Her voice trailed off.

"It's a restaurant, too. We'll be fine." I hoped I was right. The last thing I needed was to get hauled back to jail.

I was touched by her consideration until she lit a cigarette and added, "Couldn't have you thrown back in jail before you found my deranged asshole brother."

From the familiarity in the hostess' greeting, it seemed Janette was a regular here, and we were seated immediately. Waving the offered menus away she ordered for both of us. "I'll have a house salad. Dressing on the side. A vodka martini for me and," She smirked. "Water for her."

I would have killed for a chocolate martini, but I needed a clear head and to stay out of jail so I smiled back at Janette. Besides, I was still taking the antibiotics and an occasional pain pill for my arm and didn't want anything to interfere with my healing. "I'll have a diet pop instead of water."

When the waiter left, I lowered my voice. "So, what makes you think your brother had anything to do with your father's death? Especially since he was in Nepal at the time. And still is, as far as the authorities know."

She snorted. "You can't believe everything authorities say. Dylan wouldn't last a day in Nepal." She folded her arms. "Besides, I don't think I exactly said he killed my father."

"No, not in so many words, but that your brother was supposedly missing, and your father is dead. Talking on the phone, it didn't sound as if you thought it was all coincidental."

She released a put-upon sigh. "All right. I do think he's got something to do with the murder. He needs his inheritance desperately."

It was as if she'd given me a shovel, but I didn't know what I was digging for. "Okay, why does he need it so much? Drugs? Gambling?"

Her expression hardened. "Let's just say he lives extravagantly. And remember, until I talk to him, I don't want the police involved."

Too late.

She leaned in so far I could smell her face powder and

she whispered, "Who knows? Maybe he faked his trip to Nepal." Sitting back, she added, "Anyway, you have the most to lose if he's never found. So, I figured you'd search for him as if your life depended on it." She tapped her long fingernails on the table while the waiter set down our beverages.

I sipped on my pop and waited until he was out of earshot. "Assuming Dylan didn't leave the country or that he came back early, where does he hang out?"

She gulped her drink as if it were water. "He usually frequents Fun Times down in the Flats. But nobody's seen him there since the beginning of this month." She handed me a full-length photo of a guy, actually a lanky boy barely out of his teens with dark blonde hair falling into his eyes.

"This is Dylan?"

Janette raised her empty glass and twisted in her chair. "Waiter, I'd like another of these." She turned back to me. "Yes. It's the most recent one I have. So you know, I've already spoken to his girlfriend, Sarah Mueller. She insists she hasn't seen him for two weeks. Surprising since they're usually joined at the hip and he flew out only ten days ago. But, here's her name and address. Talk to her." Her mouth turned up at one corner. "Maybe you can get more out of her than Dylan's evil sister can." When I lowered my eyebrows, she added, "That's me."

I took the piece of paper just as the waiter brought Janette her second drink. She took a sip, and then with a wave of her hand, dismissed me as if I were a servant. "You can go now."

In any other circumstance I would've given her a smart retort and thrown the paper at her. Right now, though, I could ill afford to put my pride above my neck. And it was my neck on the line. I stood as if I were in total control. "I'll be in touch."

Getting back in my car, I slammed the door hard and fumed. Slowly, I forced my anger to recede and decided to chance it and call Sarah. Not surprisingly, she didn't pick up and I didn't want to leave a message. I blew out a deep, exhausted breath. I needed to go home. My body instantly relaxed. Home. My own bed. Charlie. I stepped on the gas, assuring myself he'd remember me.

I practically collided with my stepmother, Suzy, as I was entering my apartment building. She smiled. "I dropped by to feed and walk Charlie one last time. I wasn't sure if you'd be home tonight."

I was exhausted and edgy and almost snarled at one of the nicest women I knew. Instead, I pushed back on my irritability and grinned at the woman my father had been fortunate to marry. "Suzy, you've been great. I said it before, but thank you so much! I'm sure Charlie appreciated it too."

She shook her head. "The least I could do. Now, go up there and give Charlie a big hug. I know you spent some time with him already, but I don't think it was enough. That poor pup has missed you." She opened the door to the outside and shooed me in. "Go."

Pushing all the thoughts about Dylan, Sarah, and Janette out of my head, I bounded up the stairs and swung open my apartment door. There was Charlie, his front paws waving in the air. I got down to his level and threw my arms around his wiggling body. "I missed you too."

Chapter Eight

I AWOKE TO Charlie licking my face. I gently pushed him away and sat up. The fog in my brain dissipated, and I focused on my first task of the day. Find Sarah. Of course, that would be after I walked and fed Charlie.

My pet owner tasks done, I showered, took the last of my antibiotics, and wondered how to approach the girl. I also didn't want to drop the ball on the Pilkosky and Hunt angle. Somebody at that financial planning firm most likely knew something. I thought about Tommy Allegro's comment that even Dylan Morley thought there was something off about those money men.

Fully dressed, I pulled out my phone, and called Ed.

"What's up, kiddo?" He sounded hoarse, as if he'd been yelling for hours.

"Are you okay, Ed?"

He cleared his throat. "Eh, scratchy throat, headache.

Probably caught whatever's been floating around."

That put a damper on my plan. "I was going to ask you to pay a visit to Pilkosky and Hunt. Maybe find somebody willing to talk. But now, I think you should stay home and get better."

Though a rough cough, he managed, "Nah, I don't wanna sit here twiddling my thumbs. I'll do it."

I heard a patter against my windows. Rain. Aunt Lena would have my hide if I sent her sick husband out in this weather. "No, I've got a better job for you. And you can do it in your jammies." A vision of Ed in giraffe covered flannel pj's flashed through my head.

"Hmmph. For the record I don't wear pajamas, but okay. What's the job?" Another cough.

I ran through the information about Sarah and Dylan. "I need whatever there is to know about them. And where I can locate Sarah today to talk to her. Can you do that from home?"

"Sure. I'll get back to you as soon as I have something."

One final scratch behind Charlie's ear and I was out the door and in my car. With Ed sick, I had to tackle Pilkosky and Hunt myself. It was seven in the morning, so some employee could possibly be in the office. One who was willing to talk to me, if not at work, then after hours.

Traffic was fairly light and I reached my destination quicker than I'd thought. What I hadn't thought about was a burly guard in the lobby of the Pilkosky and Hunt building. He stopped me. "Ma'am I need you to sign in with your name, the time and reason for your visit."

I certainly didn't want to proclaim my wanting to shake down some Pilkosky and Hunt employee, so I hesitated. "You mean to say why I want to meet with a certain person?"

He chuckled. "No, ma'am. Just which company you're here for. Like for Medical Star or P&H. See what I mean?"

I giggled like a school girl talking to her first crush. "Oh, yes. Of course." I wrote down the required information. "Thank you for your help." Walking to the elevator, I wondered if I'd do something that would make the guard escort me from the building.

The offices of Pilkosky and Hunt were on the top floor, so I had a moment to collect my thoughts. And hope I could get the lowdown from some overworked underling who arrived at work early and left late.

The elevator doors opened and I faced a massive glass door that told me I'd arrived at my destination. I tugged hard on the handle and managed to gain enough of an entranceway to slip inside.

The reception area was unoccupied so I slowly made my way down a hall, which turned out to have nothing but closed doors on each side.

Back in the reception area, I could hear the muffled voices of a man and a woman. I headed toward the sounds and stopped at a large wooden door. Their voices were low, but I could tell by her clipped tone the woman was angry. I put my ear up against the door to hear more clearly. In the process, my purse softly banged against the wood. I held my breath, but not a second later, the door swung open. I would've probably tumbled into the room except the guy blocked my fall. And unfortunately, my view. I couldn't see the woman with whom he'd been arguing. He quickly shut the door behind him, grabbed my arms and hustled me away.

That's when I recognized him. It was Ben Pilkosky. Mr. 'I'm-Innocent-of-Embezzlement' himself.

This could be good or a disaster. I pulled myself up to my full 5'2" and thought fast." I'm Claire De—"

"Yes, yes." He waved his hand as if I were an annoying fly. "As you've no doubt heard, I'm with a client. Do you have an appointment? Never mind. Just have a seat over there." He pointed toward the receptionist's desk and frowned. "Someone will be with you…" He glanced at his Rolex watch. "Shortly." He stood like a sentry as I made my way back to the waiting area and sunk into one of the plush olive-colored chairs there.

This wasn't going as I'd thought, so I made a new plan. Instead of finding a dissatisfied corporate underling who'd spill their guts, I'd talk to that unhappy woman fighting with Pilkosky. I might even get something more on a personal level about him. When the mystery woman came out, I'd make sure to get the scoop. I only had to wait.

And wait.

The young, pretty receptionist arrived about fifteen minutes after I'd sat down. "Can I help you, ma'am?"

I approached her desk and tried to look important.

"Yes. I'm supposed to be in a conference with Mr. Pilkosky and another client. But I'm late, and I don't see the other client here."

She raised an eyebrow and looked up Pilkosky's schedule. "If you'll have a seat, I'll go find him."

She wiggled out of her chair, yanked on the hem of her formfitting mini dress and turned toward the hall. With the spiked heels she wore, it'd take her a minute to get anywhere. A minute I could use to take a quick look at Pilkosky's schedule.

I stood on my toes and tilted so far to the side I almost tipped over. Nothing on his schedule until ten in the morning. I blew out a deep breath, hoping I'd still get a chance at the mystery woman.

Not to be, though. The receptionist's scream pierced my thoughts and sent them scrambling.

Along with two men who had just arrived at work, I dashed to the room with the wooden door. The receptionist crouched against the hallway wall, sobbing and pointing at the bloody floor and Pilkosky's dead body lying on it. Though there was no weapon nearby, but it was clear he'd taken some serious blows to the head.

I took a few steps back, hoping to fade away. The last thing I needed was to be front and center on the scene of another murder. But the receptionist turned her pointing finger to me. "You! You've been here. What did you do?" Her voice rose with each word. The two men who'd flown down the hall with me blocked any escape I could have tried.

Fumbling ever so slightly, I pulled out my identification. "I'm a private investigator. That's why I wanted to talk to the deceased. Has anybody called 911?"

Chapter Nine

IT DIDN'T TAKE long for the police to show up. Nor did it take any time for my favorite police detective to arrive. Corrigan took one look at me and I'm sure, cursed under his breath. Aloud he began, "How do you do it, Claire?"

I pretended innocence. "How do I do what?"

He shoved his hands in his pockets, probably so he wouldn't be tempted to put them around my throat. "Even when you're supposed to be home, behaving yourself, you manage to get in the middle of a murder. And not just any murder." His words grew sharper. "One that could be linked to your case. Or have you forgotten you're only out because of your aunt's generosity?"

He didn't have to remind me my aunt could lose *Cannoli's*. I squinted at him and grit my teeth. "I'm trying to find who really killed Paul. What we're both trying to do. Remember? And the woman who was with Pilkosky may be it."

His face screwed up and I imagined his response wasn't going to be good humored, but he didn't get the chance. His partner, the ever gorgeous yet abhorrent to me, Abby Tilka,   interrupted us. Giving me the slightest of nods, she announced, "Brian, there's a backdoor from these offices. Locks from the inside, so somebody couldn't use it to get in, but could get out that way."

I inserted myself. "That's what I've been saying. A woman was arguing with the victim when I got here. She must've killed him then slipped out before I could see her."

Corrigan rubbed his chin. Then, to Abby, "See if there's a camera in that stairway." He turned back to me and released a deep breath and rubbed his jaw. "Okay, Claire. We'll get your statement, and then you go home. Or go visit your father. Anything, but let me do my job. If there's a connection between this murder and Paul Morley's, I swear I'll do everything I can to link them up and clear you of the murder charge." He moved in toward me, lifting his arms as if to hold me. Then, thinking better of it, he dropped them and lowered his voice. "I made you a promise, and I'll keep it."

The familiar scent of his cologne wafted into my nostrils, making me feel sort of homesick. I exhaled, as if to push any sentimentality away. "Thank you, Brian, but—" My phone went off, distracting me. It was Ed.

Corrigan warned, "There is no 'but', Claire."

Believing Ed had information on Paul's son, Dylan, and his girlfriend, I allowed Corrigan the last word and then turned away from him. "Ed, what've you got?"

Ed croaked, "Dylan's girlfriend." He cleared his throat. "She works at Westside Christian Center. You want me to go there and talk to her?" Hacking coughs followed his question.

Frowning at the phone, I answered, "Ed, thank you. Now, you sound like you should take some cough medicine and go to bed. I can take it from here."

He must have felt pretty awful, because he didn't argue. I thanked him again and we ended our conversation. I noticed, out of the corner of my eye, that Corrigan was staring at me. And not with affection.

"What've you got planned, Claire? A trip to Nepal?"

Sweetness dripped from my mouth, "Of course not. Don't you know I can't leave the country?"

He fumed and looked ready to verbally rein me in when he got a call. He commanded me not to move, but I displayed my impatience by tapping my foot. His phone conversation ended quickly, and Corrigan's attention was back on me. "Your cellmate, Nadia, was released on bail late last night. Looks like we might have a perp. Complete with motive and opportunity."

My hands clenched. Nadia claimed Ben Pilkosky had framed her. No doubt she was full of rage toward him. Was she the woman arguing with himthis morning? I swallowed and chose my words carefully. "She couldn't have been foolish enough to come see the victim."

Corrigan snickered. "Yeah, I bet she's a real genius."

Abby returned and we didn't discuss it any further. "We got footage from the security camera. A woman in a hooded coat went down the stairs. We couldn't see her face, though."

Corrigan acknowledged the find and then, having morphed back into his official detective role addressed me. "Okay. I think I've got everything I need from you, Claire. You can go now."

I hated that his stiff, authoritative detective self had dismissed me. But, I reasoned, it gave me the chance to get to the Westside Christian Center. Maybe Sarah Mueller could donate some information about her boyfriend, Dylan.

All the way there, I thought up snappy, snarky things I should have said to Corrigan. I finally reached the Center and had just found a parking spot when my phone rang.

Nadia.

I rubbed my face and debated on letting it go to voicemail. But my Girl Scout sense of right and wrong, charity versus…well, that's it. I answered. "This is Claire."

"This is Nadia. You know, we were cellmates. We shared those nasty jailhouse meals." She paused. "Thank God you answered!"

My shoulders rose and I could feel my body stiffen. I responded, using my most formal tone. "Yes. I, um remember. How are you?" *Stupid question.* She probably just offed Pilkosky.

"Doing fine, now. Someone posted my bail. Beats me who the hell would do it. Wasn't you, was it?"

"No. Sorry." Trying to keep my voice casual, I asked, "Um, so what did you do this morning?" I could tip off Corrigan.

"Slept in my own bed. Best night's sleep I've gotten in a while. Why?"

I kept it friendly. "Just wondering how you spent your first night as a free woman." She still could've risen early and made it to Pilkosky's office before I got there. "Did you have something for breakfast that wasn't the slop they fed us in the prison cafeteria?" I wondered if she'd know I was texting Corrigan while we talked. I needed to get to him.

She chortled, "Yeah, I made myself some coffee and toast. And, I didn't have to worry about breaking a tooth on anything." She got serious quickly. "Never mind that, though. Listen, that slimeball, Pilkosky's gotta own up to what he did. I'm gonna fix it so he does."

I paused, puzzled. If she didn't already know someone had 'fixed' Pilkosky, maybe she wasn't the mystery woman in his office.

Impatiently, she added, "Are you with me so far, Claire?"

"Go on. You didn't call just to gab." My mind was spinning so fast it could've been producing sparks.

"You're a PI and I need your help to squeeze the truth out of him."

Unless she was covering her tracks, she didn't know. "Nadia, Ben Pilkosky is dead. Somebody killed him this morning."

"Dammit! Now, I'll never get the truth out of him. Who did it?"

I squeezed my eyes shut and silenced my brain so I could listen to what my gut said. "They don't know, but—"

Her voice rose. "But they'll come after me for sure. What a crappy time for me to get out."

My gut starting screaming she was innocent. "Maybe somebody timed it that way."

"Ya mean to pin it on me? Who would hate me that much?"

"I don't know." I dismissed calling Corrigan. Nadia didn't kill Pilkosky, though she might have been capable of it. "The police should be able to find out though."

"Yeah, and they've always bent over backwards to help me." She dropped the sarcasm and pleaded, "Now you've gotta help me. Meet with me, please."

All I needed was to get involved in another murder. I tapped my hand on the steering wheel. I shouldn't do it, but she didn't kill Pilkosky, I was sure of it. And, what if his death had something to do with Paul's murder? I swallowed hard. "All right." Though I knew our meeting could be permanently cancelled if the police got to her before I did. "There's something I've got to do first. And, you need to get a *good* lawyer. Write this name down. Harold Goldfarb. He's creepy, but he'll help you." I gave her his number. "I'll call you this afternoon. I promise."

I heard pounding, as on a door. She snorted, "Cops didn't waste any time." She ended the call.

Chapter Ten

I BIT THE OUTSIDE of my lower lip, wondering if I should try to intervene with the police and Nadia. I rationalized that it was better to let Goldfarb deal with it. I had to pursue proving my own innocence.

While I'd been driving to the Westside Christian Center, I murmured a prayer that I'd find the information to make that happen. And I believed that information had much to do with Dylan Morley.

I made my way through a mix of men and women who looked as if they'd fallen on hard times. I kept my head down to avoid eye contact with any of them.

Once inside the Center's open and sparsely furnished waiting/reception area, I asked a woman standing alone if she knew where to find Sarah Mueller. Revealing teeth that hadn't seen a dentist in years, she pointed at a hallway on the left. "She's over there. Tall, blonde lady."

I found my way to the end of the hallway and toward

Sarah, who was busy piling clothes into separate heaps. She was, indeed, blonde. A golden shade that, as a child, I'd wished I had. Not that it would've looked good with my dark eyebrows, but I didn't care.

"Excuse me. Are you Sarah Mueller?"

She didn't even look up from the current stack she sorted. "If you want to volunteer or make a donation, you need to call ahead."

"No, it's neither." I placed my hand flat upon the pile. "My name is Claire. I'm a private investigator and I have some questions."

Her head shot up. For a second, I was taken aback. She closely resembled a work-out Barbie Doll. Her arms were well toned and her blue eyes, pert nose and glowing complexion had to be courtesy of a mad plastic surgeon attempting perfection. I blinked and that thought fled from my mind as she practically screamed, "You're the woman charged with Mr. Morley's murder!"

I should've been used to hearing that, but it took me a second. Then, "I didn't kill anyone. I'm looking for his *real* killer. That's why I'm here. You see—"

She waved my protest away and hissed though perfect teeth, "You need to leave. Right now. I have nothing to say to you."

I stood my ground. "Where is Dylan Morley?"

"He's in Nepal. I don't know when he'll get back."

She wasn't a very good liar. Her face turned a rosier color, and she hid her shaky hands beneath the closest clothes pile.

Taking advantage of her discomfort, I leaned over, my face near hers. "Come on, Sarah. You know where he is. It's not really Nepal, is it?"

She shook her head hard and her hair bounced around her pretty face.

"This lady bothering you, Miss Sarah?" I turned toward the voice. It belonged to a man whose eyes clearly showed his adoration for the woman. To my dismay, he was roughly the size of a mountain.

Sarah took a deep breath, no doubt relieved by her imminent rescue. All feminine honey, "Thank you, Luther. The lady was just leaving."

I smiled my most charming smile and used my sweetest voice. "Hello, Luther." I pulled out my photo of Dylan. "I'm Claire, and I was just asking Sarah if her boyfriend, Dylan, has been around here lately."

His brow furrowed as if trying to recall a long ago incident. "Oh, yeah. Didn't he go far away, like to Naples?"

Sarah jumped in. "Nepal." Pointedly, she added, "And he's there now."

I put up my hands in surrender. "Okay. Thank you both. I'm leaving now." I backed away, my eyes on both of them, until I reached the hall entrance. Then I turned around and, what seemed like a millisecond, Luther appeared beside me. "I'll walk ya out." His tone didn't leave me any room to disagree.

The earthy aroma of stewed vegetables and meat hit me the instant we got to the large reception area. On the other side of the area was a kitchen with a rope across its entrance.

At the glass door leading to outside, a hoard of men and women were queuing up for their daily meal courtesy of the Center's ladies in the kitchen. Smelling whatever was cooking reminded me I hadn't eaten anything since that stale brownie I scarfed down before I left that morning.

Luther turned his head and noisily inhaled, let out a sigh, and held the door open for me. Hoping my escort would stop there, I said, "Okay, Luther. You don't need to walk me to my car. Especially since it looks like mealtime."

He shook his head. "Nah, Miss Sarah would want me to take you all the way out." He looked at the line forming and without turning back to me said, "Come on, let's go."

My eyes followed his. The line was getting longer and more restless with people jostling for a place. One of them was a thin young man, with dirty blonde hair pushing his way toward the front of the line.

I stopped for a better look, but Luther was having none of it. "Keep going. I want it so's you don't come back and bother Miss Sarah again. She's such a nice lady."

I dug my heels in. "Wait. I see someone I might know." *Dylan?*

Luther scratched his temple. "Uh," He set his jaw. "You're trying to fool me. Keep moving."

Knowing if I protested too vigorously, the young man I wanted to scope out more closely might figure out what was going on and bolt. "Fine. I'm walking to my car. See?" I pointed at my vehicle and continued toward it, figuring I'd drive away and then circle back once Luther left.

He folded his tattooed arms and leaned back on his heels while I unlocked my door. "And don't you come back." He actually watched me get inside and start the engine. Only then did he turn away.

I slammed my car into reverse and zipped around the corner, holding my breath until I got back to the Westside Christian Center. Luther had disappeared, but so had the young man who might have been Dylan.

Throwing caution to the wind, I spun into a parking space and dashed back inside the Center, hoping against hope the guy I wanted to check out was still there.

No sign of him. "Damn, damn, double damn." I cut through the gang that was still in line, earning some not-so-nice names and a couple jabs to my ribs. But I made it to the front.

A plump, middle-aged woman in a hair net crossed her arms and eyed me critically. "Everyone has to wait their turn or they don't get fed."

I held up my hands and spoke fast, before the now angry crowd attacked. "I'm a private detective. I need some information. Please." She looked to the ceiling, blew out a put-open breath, and nodded. I flashed Dylan's photo and asked if she'd seen him.

She shrugged. "Nope."

Not willing to give up, I asked her about the young

man I'd seen in line.

She snorted and raised her chin at the men still in line. "It could be any one of them. Sorry. You'll have to move along."

The guy behind me pressed against me and mumbled, "Get outta the way 'fore I move you out."

His threat along with the smell of booze, sweat, and unwashed clothes made my choice easy. I stepped out of line, feeling as if I were the donkey seeing the carrot dangling in front of me, but unable to grab on to it.

In the parking lot, I spotted a man in an ill-fitting overcoat too heavy for the current weather pacing behind my car. Not knowing if he had carjacking in mind, I yelled at him to step away.

He stopped and faced me, growling, "Hey, keep it down." He dropped his voice. "I got information."

Cautiously, I stepped toward him. "About?"

He cast his eyes around. "The guy you're lookin' for." He held out his palm, but it wasn't to check if it was raining.

I silently calculated the amount of cash I had on me. "What about him?"

The stranger narrowed his eyes, shoving his outstretched hand closer to me.

I placed a folded five-dollar bill into his hand. "Okay. What can you tell me?"

He looked down at the money and then snorted, "You're kidding. Ain't you got more than that?"

I almost blurted out that I didn't, but decided instead

to play it cagey. "Depends on the information."

He wasn't buying. "Lemme see the rest of the money first."

Puffing my chest out, I countered with, "I've got it. But, how do I know you've got information worth more?"

Shrugging, he quickly pocketed the money in hand and then glanced around. "Come on back here at four. The guy you want'll be here, sniffin' around that Sarah chick."

"Thanks. That should help." I turned to get into my car.

"Hey, wait a minute." He put a firm hand on my shoulder and snarled, "I gave you good information. Now, I want more than that crummy ten."

Not wanting to create a scene or have him injure me, I nodded. "Okay." Again, I dug into my purse, but found nothing more than two sticks of gum and an unused plastic bandage. Luckily, underneath those I struck gold. Or, maybe just gold-plate. I handed him a five-dollar gift card to a nearby burger place. "It's the best I can do. You can get a double patty with this."

He groaned. "What the hell." He grabbed it and stomped off.

Before he could change his mind and come after me, I hopped into my car and started it up. I had a couple hours before I needed to be back, so debated where to best spend my time.

My stomach released a growl that would've put any wild king-of-the-beast's to shame. That made my decision easier. *Cannoli's.* I could have just stopped at a fast food restaurant and then continued on my quest to find Paul Morley's killer, but, I'd given away my gift card and money. Besides, I rationalized something sweet would provide carbs to help my brain work faster and more efficiently.

Chapter Eleven

CANNOLI'S WAS HOPPING when I got there. Angie, my aunt's best friend and long-time employee, was working hard. Her fingers were flying, making change and packing bakery boxes with luscious cakes and pastries.

In between, she tilted her head toward the kitchen. "Go on back. You look hungry so go eat. Keep up your strength."

I nodded, a tiny bit disappointed she hadn't said that I looked too skinny. I glanced down at my hips. If only stress could burn fat!

Aunt Lena was manning the kitchen, pulling cookies from the oven and loading them onto cooling trays. "Glad you're here. Now, if you work, you eat."

Between mouthfuls of two double chocolate chip cookies with chocolate icing smashed between them, I told her about chasing after Dylan Morley.

She wiped her hands on her apron and stopped

stacking cooled pastries. "So, you think he killed his father? For his fortune?" She shook her head and tsk'd, "Thank God we don't have that kind of money." She made the Sign of the Cross. "Better not to be rich than to have kids who hate you."

My phone went off. It was Nadia. In my quest to find Dylan, I'd forgotten about her being arrested. Guilt made me answer. "Nadia. Are you okay?"

Her voice thick with anger. "Of course I'm not. I'm in jail again." She took a breath. "Look, you promised to help me."

I ignored my aunt's waving hand as she tried to get my attention. "Yes. I will. I'm, um, trying to figure out Dylan Morley's part in his father's and Pilkosky's death. Have you called the lawyer I told you about?"

"Yeah. Says he'll be here 'shortly'. Whatever *that* means."

I squeezed my eyes shut, willing Goldfarb to get there quickly. "Okay. The minute I get something, I'll let you know through him. I promise. It'll be all right." I coughed as if that reassurance had wanted to stick in my throat.

I could hear someone on her end ordering her to end the call. To have something to do, I picked up a cupcake I'd set my sights on earlier and took a bite.

My aunt's eyes were on me like a hungry man's on a steak. "Who was that?"

I gave her an abbreviated version. "A client I promised to help. She's in a lot of trouble."

Aunt Lena shook her head. "It's good that you take

care of strangers. But, you know, God blesses children who love their folks the best."

I eyed her suspiciously, "Okaay…"

She turned back to the cooling cookies and murmured, "It's great to help other people who need it, but your family, especially your father, needs attention."

I set the cupcake down. "Is he sick?" My stomach roiled. Not illness on top of a jailbird daughter who owes him so much, including some of my bail. Remorse heavy as loaded cement trucks rolled over me.

My next words spewed from deep within me. "I promise to make sure my dad gets his money back so he can pay for whatever care he needs." I grabbed her hand. "And I'll do whatever I can so you don't lose *Cannoli's*."

She gave my hand a squeeze and then extricated hers. "Don't worry about me or paying your father back. Not yet, anyway. Although we'd both rest better if you'd find that lawyer's real killer. No. There's something else going on with Frank." Her face scrunched up. "It's killing me I can't figure it out."

"I'll see what I can find out." I had plenty on me, but now, it seemed my dad not only had debt because of me, something else was bothering him. What if he was sick? Really sick?

The cupcake no longer looked appealing and I pushed it out of sight. "I've got another hour before I have somewhere to be. I'll go talk to Dad."

Aunt Lena kissed my cheek. I smelled vanilla. "You're a good girl. Now go. And let me know what's going on."

Walking to my car, an avalanche of feelings nearly knocked me over; two murders that may or may not be related, my staying out of prison and not having my father and Aunt Lena lose everything. Now promising to help Nadia was just one more snowflake.

I arrived at my father's place in a daze, unable to remember exactly how I got there.

Suzy greeted me with a smile and a pan of bubbling lasagna. "Come on in, Claire! We're eating early so I can get back to the salon. Lots of clients this evening." She beamed with pride. Since opening her own hair salon, she'd become a successful businesswoman.

My stomach was still in a pretzel shape, but nonetheless I plastered on a smile. "That smells great." A pause then, "Is my dad home?"

"He just got back. He's in the bedroom changing clothes." She lowered her voice. "You know, his sixtieth birthday is next month. I'm planning a surprise party for him. I'll fill you in later, but I may need your help, assuming you're, um, not, um…"

I finished her sentence. "In jail."

She gave me a sympathetic smile and then turned her head toward the bedroom and yelled, "Frank, lasagna's ready and Claire's here!"

My dad came into the kitchen and flung his arms out. "Hey, Pumpkin!"

I'd just seen him yesterday, but I walked into his hug. "Hi, Dad."

Into my hair, he spoke, "Glad you came to see the old

man."

I took a step back. I was sadly shocked. He'd always told me age was just a number you could add to or subtract from, depending on how you felt that day. "Old? You're not old. You're in the prime of your life."

Setting an additional plate on the table, Suzy murmured, "Frank, this really isn't the time. Claire's got enough to deal with. Come on everyone. Sit down before the lasagna gets cold."

My dad pulled out a chair for me and then for himself while Suzy, standing, cut into the lasagna. He lowered his head a bit and said nothing more.

I had to know what the issue was. Aunt Lena demanded it and I was getting worried. Yet this could be like sticking my hand into a hornet's nest. Since it was for my father, though, I stuck it in all the way. "It's okay, Dad. I want to hear what's wrong."

"Nah, we can talk about it some other time." He fanned out his napkin. "Okay, let's eat."

Not wanting to let it go and knowing Aunt Lena would be all over me, I opened my mouth to egg him on. One whopper of a warning look from Suzy told me I'd be treading where only fools dared. Much as I wanted to find out, I figured it'd be best to bide my time.

Squares of noodles, cheese and tomato sauce oozing from all sides, sat in front of us, but we waited until Suzy sat down. Helping herself to some grated Parmigiano-Reggiano cheese, she asked, "Have there been any new leads in your case, Claire?"

Looking up from my plate, I responded with, "As a matter of fact, I'm tracking down what could be a very revealing lead."

My dad set his fork down firmly. "Maybe you should let the police handle it."

It was my turn to lay my utensil down. I struggled to keep my voice level. "By police, do you mean Brian?" My teeth clenched. "Have you talked to him?"

Looking everywhere but at me, my dad nodded. "He called this morning. Wanted to make sure we weren't worrying. He's a really good guy. The kind you don't find around every corner."

I carefully wiped my mouth. "What did he say?"

"That he was gonna find out who really killed that lawyer. He knows it wasn't you." He took a bite of lasagna and mumbled, "After he does, you two should get back together. I don't understand why you broke up in the first place. He still loves you, ya know."

The big block of worry in my chest dissolved knowing the issue with my dad wasn't illness. Then a twinge of irritation hit me. "Is that what's bothering you? Brian and me splitting up?"

"Frank…" Suzy placed her hand lightly on my dad's forearm.

I shoved my chair back from the table and raised both my hands as if I was pushing against a brick wall. "It's okay, Suzy. Let him speak his peace." Not that I really wanted to hear more, but he's my dad and I was in his home.

With an exaggerated, thank you, he went on. "Claire Marie, I've never interfered with who you chose in your romantic life. Even with that *sgradevole* dental student. I knew he wasn't for you. But I didn't say anything until he broke your heart. Then I wanted to," Dad's hands turned to fists that he rotated as if bending a stick. "break his neck."

I merely nodded, knowing there was more to come.

"Brian's the first decent guy you've let close to you since then. We all hoped…" He shook his head, "but no, you got cold feet and dumped him. For what? A guy who mixes cement?" He wasn't done. "If you'd stayed with Brian, you wouldn't be in this mess…" His voice trailed off.

My father's words stung me deeply. If a heart could cry, mine would have drowned in its own tears. I drew in a deep breath and sprang from my chair and would have dashed from the room, even from the house, without a look back, but his strong hand grabbed my arm.

"Claire, honey," He hung his head. "I'm sorry. Sit down. I'm just worried about you."

Tightlipped, I again lowered myself into my chair and I crossed my arms protectively.

"Pumpkin, I love you, you should know that. Whatever you do, I support. It's only that I hoped you'd be settled by now. Maybe even thinking about giving me a grandkid. I know. It's just an old man's wishful thinking. It's my dream. Maybe not yours." He heaved a sigh. "But I'll get past it. Give me time. I support you and whatever you need."

I lowered my eyelids and shook my head. "I know, Dad." *Grandkids?* I rubbed my face. Maybe at one time that would've been possible, but not now. *Maybe not ever.*

He spread his hands out on the table, and I noticed for the first time a few grey hairs on them. I reached out and hugged him. "I love you too." I squeezed hard. "Ferociously. And I'll get through this and then we'll see what happens. Who knows? Maybe Brian and I will get back together." *When chocolate truffles reproduce.*

Right now, there was no sense explaining why Brian and I broke up. It wasn't anybody's fault. *Not exactly.* I blew out a breath, glancing at the clock on their dining room wall. I wanted to spend more time here, with my father and Suzy. Where I felt loved, although not quite approved of. But I needed to get back to the Christian Center. I took a hurried bite out of my now cool lasagna. Then I jumped up and grabbed my purse. "I've gotta go. I'm going to find someone who may be able to clear me of the murder. Thank you for dinner. Love you both."

My dad said, "You be careful. You want me to call Brian to help you?"

My answer was firm. "No."

Suzy popped up, ever the gracious host. "You want some lasagna to take home?"

I hustled to the door. "It was delicious, but no thanks." I hoped I could make it in time.

Driving back to the Westside Christian Center, I tried keeping my mind on finding Dylan, but it kept wandering back to Corrigan and my father's comments. I shook my head a few times to clear it. Breaking up with him couldn't have possibly been because I was afraid. Out loud I proclaimed, "I've conquered my fears." *Or had I just buried them?*

Chapter Twelve

LOST IN MY thoughts, I got to the Center before I realized it. I parked and forbade any Corrigan thoughts to invade my head while I tracked down Dylan Morley.

I patted my purse to make sure I had identification. Being out on bail, I shouldn't have had a gun, but I didn't relish the idea of being defenseless either. So I made sure it lay securely within my reach.

The Center served breakfast and lunch only, so those who'd been hanging about earlier had already dispersed. As a volunteer there, though, Sarah might still be around. And, if the man who'd taken my money was right, Dylan could be with her. I knew I was playing the odds, but I was running out of options.

Luckily, the doors to the Center remained open. Making sure nobody saw me I slipped inside and surveyed the now dimly lit lobby. A much brighter light shone down the hallway where I first encountered Sarah.

I tiptoed halfway down that hallway and was rewarded with hearing a man yelling, "Come on, Sarah. We gotta hurry."

Moving quietly forward, I peeked around the edge of the doorframe and spotted a scruffier and thinner-looking Dylan Morley. Delight that I'd found him mixed with worry when I didn't see Sarah. No matter.

Wherever they were heading, I needed to stop them. Catching him would draw her out, I was sure. I pulled my gun out to better persuade him to come along, but banged my elbow on the hall railing. The pain rippled down my arm and I almost dropped my weapon.

Ignoring my throbbing elbow, I leaped from the shadows and bellowed, "Dylan Morley! Hands in the air!"

He placed a heavy looking knapsack on a nearby bench and put his hands out, palms facing me, in front. "It's cool. Don't shoot." The quiver in his voice betraying his nervousness.

Using my most official voice, I added, "I'm a private investigator and I'm calling the police to arrest you."

He dropped his hands. "What for?"

I waved my gun. "Put your hands up in the air." Once he complied, I continued, "You faked your trip to Nepal so you could kill your own father. Now, tell me where—"

He cut me off. "Wait! I'm innocent. I swear. I can explain."

My instincts told me he should save it for the cops, but curiosity won over good sense. "Okay, make it quick and keep your hands up high."

"Look, I didn't kill my dad. Yeah, okay, I faked my trip to Nepal. I had to get away from my sister, Janette. Sure, I want my inheritance, but not the way she does. She'd murder me for it. She probably killed my father to get her hands on it quicker. Can't you see? I'm a dead man if I stay here."

My brain began to spin and I bit my lower lip. Janette had employed me to find her brother, claiming he was the killer. Was that a ploy to throw me off? Who's telling the truth, the brother or the sister? What if neither is? I shook the questions out of my mind. This wasn't the moment to decide. I'd let the cops sort out the truth.

I must have looked a bit confused because Dylan seemed to believe he could play with my head, and slyly inched toward me. I wasn't that distracted, though. "That's far enough. Where's Sarah?"

Unfortunately, my attention turned toward a noise behind me. It was only for a second, but that was enough. Dylan grabbed his knapsack off the bench and threw it at me, knocking me off balance. The gun fell from my hand and he and I scrambled for it. He was faster and stronger.

Now, Dylan pointed my weapon at me.

Sarah, who'd been standing just inside the doorway, walked toward Dylan. "What's going on?" She eyed me. "You were here before asking about Dylan. Who are you?"

Before I could answer, Dylan growled, "Grab her purse, Sarah. That'll tell us who she is."

Sarah ripped my bag from my shoulder and dug

through it until she found my identification. Her eyes narrowed. "You told me your name was Claire, but nothing about you being the one charged with killing Dylan's father!"

Tables now reversed, it was my turn to proclaim my innocence. "I didn't—"

"Shut up!" Dylan's spittle flew with the force of his words. With the gun in his hand, he motioned toward the closet. "Get in there."

My stomach sank as they bolted the door to the tiny closet, which locked from the outside. I banged on it to no avail. Ten, fifteen minutes passed. *Think, Claire.* I longed for Ed's burglar tools. As it was, I didn't even have a hair pin. They'd taken my phone, so I couldn't call anyone. I suddenly wished I'd gone to the bathroom before coming to the Center. The cramped closet was so small there wasn't room to sit, so I leaned up against a rubber trash receptacle, expecting a long night.

Losing track of time was easy, but thankfully, finally, I heard footsteps outside the closet door. Through dry lips, I shouted, "Help! I'm locked inside the closet!"

The door swung open and I rushed out, almost knocking down a uniformed cop. "Whoa!" He pushed me back just a bit. "I'm Officer Wagner. A call came in claiming someone was locked up in here."

I suppressed the urge to kiss his hand. "Yes. Thank you!"

He frowned. "You work here?"

I took a step back. "No, but I swear I wasn't

trespassing." I hurried on, "I need to talk to Detective Brian Corrigan right away. I've got some important information about a case he's working."

The cop's bushy brows furrowed. "Hey, aren't you the lady who killed that lawyer?" He crossed his arms over his protruding belly.

"Allegedly. But I'm innocent and the information I just obtained can prove it." I made a move toward my purse. "Now, if you don't mind, I'm going to call Detective Corrigan."

The cop blocked my path and snarled, "I do mind. What were you doing here and how did you get locked in the closet?" He pulled out a notepad.

I dug my nails into the palms of my hands to stop from screaming at this guy. Dylan and Sarah already had a head start. Now even more time would be lost because of this dunderhead. I put my hands together, prayer-like, "I'll answer all your questions. Even ones you don't ask, but please, please let me make my phone call first."

He scratched his forehead. "Okay, I guess I'll let you do that. But no funny business, hear?"

I let out a deep breath. "Loud and clear. Thank you." I punched in Corrigan's number, praying he'd pick up.

My prayer was answered. Knowing full well that shortly he'd be chastising me, I lost no time in filling him in.

The man never disappointed. His first words were, "What the hell were you thinking?" Followed quickly by, "Did they give any clues where they were headed?"

"No, but I bet one of them called the cops to get me released. Probably Sarah. If you can trace that call, you'll find them." I mentally crossed my fingers hoping that would be true.

Officer Wagner, no doubt feeling left out of the loop, wrested my phone from me. "This is Officer Wagner. Who am I talking to?" His scowl disappeared. "Detective Corrigan." He paused, listening. "Yes, sir. I was gonna take her in for trespassing. At my precinct."

Corrigan's voice boomed through the phone and Wagner's shoulders drooped. "I understand, sir. All right. She's still coming with me to the station, but I'll wait for you before I do anything."

I didn't dare show an 'I told you so' smirk and I did my best to keep it out of my voice. "I'll be happy to accompany you to the station now, Officer."

His teeth gritted, "Yeah, well, we'll see what happens next."

My only hope was that Dylan and Sarah, the kid's modern-day version of Bonnie Parker, would be caught next.

Chapter Thirteen

IT TOOK CORRIGAN forty-five minutes to arrive at the station and then another hour to get me released. I didn't have to ask how he managed that. The minute we were outside the station and safely away from curious eyes and ears, he dropped his frustration on top of me.

His face turned a slightly redder version than I ever recalled. "Do you know the number of favors I had to call in to get you released?" Without waiting for a response, he yelled, "I'm going to be indebted for the rest of my natural life! All because you can't leave anything alone." He dropped his voice and grabbed both of my forearms. "I get it. You don't have any faith in me. You think you're the only person who cares about proving your innocence."

The hurt in his eyes confused me and a weird feeling of shame crawled through my stomach. "I do believe in you, Brian. It's just…" I shook my head, trying to find the right words. "You're right. I can't leave it alone." I plastered a fake Joker-style smile on my face. "And look, I did find Dylan. I admit, I lost him again, but we know now he didn't go to Nepal. Or anywhere. Doesn't that mean that he should be a person-of-interest?" I pressed my hands onto my hips. "Well?"

"We'll continue this in the car." Corrigan roughly escorted me to where he'd parked. "Get in. I'll drive you back." When we were both seated, he rubbed his face hard. "Look, Claire, you're getting what you want. Dylan Morley's whereabouts are being investigated as we speak." He raised his index finger and pointed it at my nose. "But you stay out of it. Go to *Cannoli's* and help your aunt. Or, or drop in on your father and eat pasta with him. Anything, but stay out of this."

Corrigan's mentioning my father brought back this afternoon's conversation over lasagna with him. A stab of guilt hit me, and I didn't like it. I wanted to change the subject, and at the same time, put Corrigan on the defensive. I brought up his recent call to my father. "That call to my dad was totally unnecessary."

He sniffed. "You're wrong there. The poor guy is worried sick about you. I wanted him to know I would do everything I could to get you free."

I tsk'd. He was right. And a better person would appreciate that he'd done that. I wanted to be a better person. "Actually, that was really considerate of you." I couldn't help but add, "Except now, he's thinking about us getting back together. Even having kids." I would have chuckled with my last sentence, but the wistful look on Corrigan's face stopped me.

He covered it up quickly. "Yeah, well, I guess he's at that age when having grandkids seems important. A legacy, you know?"

My phone buzzed before I could say anything else. Which was probably a good thing since putting my foot in my mouth was usually followed by me opening my mouth wider and putting in the other.

I held the phone away from my ear. "It's Harold, my lawyer."

Corrigan turned his attention back onto the road.

"Claire, it's me, Harold Goldfarb, your attorney. First, thank you for my new client, not that I can disclose any information about her case. Attorney-client privilege." He cleared his throat. "Be that as it may, I believe you and my new client have something in common. One dead financial planner, Benjamin Pilkosky."

I sucked in an impatient breath. "I understand. Now, have you found anything to help me?"

"I just learned that the victim's absent son is now on the radar and was on the run. Perhaps he has information on his father's death."

I closed my eyes and gritted my teeth. "He may well have, Harold. Do you know if the son's been brought in yet?"

Harold stammered, "N-no. I'm sorry, I don't." He paused. "I probably should get back to my new client. Oh, I almost forgot. She wanted me to remind you of your promise to her."

Groaning, I acknowledged that promise. "I'll do what I can for her." I ended the call before Harold had a chance to irritate me even more. Besides, we had arrived at the Westside Christian Center's parking lot.

Corrigan watched me fumble for my keys. "Who did you promise to help?"

Feeling I had nothing to lose by telling him, I confessed, "One of my cellmates, Nadia. Somebody anonymously posted bail for her and then killed the guy Nadia swore she'd bring down."

That tiny vein in Corrigan's temple be-bopped. "You're talking about Pilkosky and that woman who was busted for embezzling? My sweet Lord, aren't you in enough trouble without jumping into another murder investigation?"

Having no snarky answer, actually no answer at all, I opened the car door and started getting out.

"Claire." He took my arm to stop me. "I'm determined to help you any way I can, but if you go down this rabbit hole, I may not be able to follow you."

"And save me?" Anger fueled by my uncertainty of what I was doing pulsed through me. "I don't need saving. Do you hear me?"

Face pinched, he withdrew his hand. "Yeah."

"Fine."

Aping me with arms crossed, he repeated, "Fine."

I laughed. Seeing the shocked look on Corrigan's face, I roared with laughter until I struggled to catch my breath.

Totally inappropriate.

He scowled. "What's so funny?"

Dabbing at my eyes, I exhaled and responded, "Not sure." I swallowed and shook my head. "Right now everything I touch seems to turn out wrong. And look at us. How no matter what, we're still fighting and we're not even together anymore. How did we ever think we could make it work?" I started laughing again, but this time it seemed emptier and rather sad.

Without a word, Corrigan leaned over and kissed me, hard. To my dismay, my body responded and I didn't pull away.

His blue eyes bore into me. "That's how we make it work, Claire."

I closed my eyes. "I'd be the last to deny the physical attraction. But, that's not enough. If I get out of this mess and ever find the right partner, it'll be somebody who respects me. Someone who admires and is even proud of what I've accomplished."

Unwilling for him to see me morph into an emotional lump, I opened my eyes but turned away.

"Claire, I'm just trying to—"

"Besides, what about the enchanting Abby and your mutual attraction?"

He waved his hand in dismissal. "That was a nonstarter from the get-go. And I—"

I put up my own hand now to stop him. "I've gotta go." Once again I opened the car door and slid out. This time, Corrigan didn't stop me.

Pride battled my desire to hop back into his car. I shook my head. *Nothing's different than before.* Sure, if I allowed it, we might start again. But then what? Besides, right now, too many pieces of me were scattered about. I couldn't devote even the tiniest of them to whatever that was in Corrigan's car.

Chewing on my lower lip, I forced my emotions to take a back seat and, once his car pulled away, I made a call.

"This is Janette Morley. Hello, Claire." She sniffed. "I wondered when you'd get around to calling me. I hear you've been very busy, discovering yet another dead body."

I wondered silently if she was responsible for both deaths, and was about to demand a meeting with her to explore that possibility right away.

She beat me to it. "You talked to my brother, Dylan." Not a question.

"Yes. Yes, I did." I kept my tone neutral, hoping I could handle this dynamite without getting blown up. "I'd like to meet with you and discuss that."

"I imagine you would." She paused. "All right. Let's meet at the Tango Room, where we met before. You know, keep it nice and public. Be there tonight at eleven."

She ended the call before I could say another word.

It was nine o'clock and I already felt as if I'd been beaten against a rock. I needed something to perk me up. Charlie, my sweet dog, popped into my mind like a cold bottle of beer does to a hot, thirsty man.

ജ

CHARLIE WAS JUST AS HAPPY to see me as I was to see him. His rear end wiggling back and forth in happiness and excitement cheered me as nothing, even chocolate, could. We went out for a quick walk and while he sniffed around and did his business, I mentally reviewed everything I'd heard or seen since the day Paul died, discarding what I believed was unimportant. I was still left with a big pile of something resembling what Charlie was dropping.

My pup and I returned to my apartment, and I took off his leash. He quickly flipped over to his back to get a belly rub, and I absently complied while I plotted how to approach my meeting with Janette.

Blowing out a deep breath, I wished, not for the first time, to be like Charlie. A chewy toy and a rub were all he needed to be satisfied.

Chapter Fourteen

I ARRIVED AT THE Tango Room on time, but Janette wasn't there. The young, shapely hostess in a skin tight mini dress seated me by the kitchen. I guess I didn't look classy enough for a good table.

Janette made her entrance a few minutes later. Like a queen with her courtiers, she greeted other customers with a regal nod. Arriving at my table though, she eyed me up and down. "You look terrible."

I grimaced, realizing I had no makeup on and my clothes were covered with dog hairs. "Good to see you too. Have a seat and let's get down to business."

Once seated, she waved the approaching waitress away, yet managed to keep her eyes on me. "Yes, let's do. Why hasn't my brother been arrested? Was it your incompetence that allowed him to escape?"

I dug my nails into the tablecloth so I wouldn't dig them into her expertly made-up eyes. I forced my voice to stay level. "You know, it's funny. He claims he's innocent. In fact, he thinks you're out to get him and that you killed your father."

She scoffed. "And you believe someone who faked his own disappearance and once caught in his lie blames his sister?"

This wasn't going quite the way I'd wanted. "Just so I know. Where were you when your father was killed?"

Her eyes flashed. "You must be kidding!" When I didn't respond, she huffed, "Very well. I was at a benefit brunch for the Murray Hill Preservation." She motioned the waitress over and then added, "I'm surprised you didn't know that. After all, that detective with the stunning blue eyes already interviewed me."

Dismissing her comment about Corrigan, I countered with, "But I'm sure you could have snuck out at some time, killed your dad and returned, nobody the wiser."

She looked at me as if I were the dumbest being alive. "Return covered in blood? And nobody noticing? Come on, Claire, even you can do better than that." Her eyebrows knit. "Or maybe you actually did kill my father and are trying to put it on me." Her voice turned philosophical. "Not that my father didn't deserve what he got, but after talking with you, I doubt you'd be capable of it…"

I opened my mouth to argue, but I was so angry and frustrated, I knew I wouldn't be able to match her viciousness. So, I bit my lip and bided my time.

The waitress came to take our orders, a dirty martini

for Janette and, because after a day like today, I'd earned it, a chocolate martini for me.

Once we were alone again, Janette peered at me and I knew she wasn't finished tearing me down. "On top of everything else, why would I hire you to find my brother if I killed my father?" She tsk'd and shook her head. "I'm afraid you're not thinking straight. My father made a lot of enemies, with his dishonesty and self-absorption. Just ask my mother." She must have noted my eyebrows shooting up because she added, "Don't even think it. My dear mother is permanently ensconced in Tuscany. She and her current flame, Rosano, are enjoying the very generous divorce settlement she received from Daddy."

Our drinks were placed in front of us and I took a long gulp, almost gagging from the strength of the alcohol. Ignoring the burning in my throat, I choked out, "Is there anyone else with a motive to kill your father?"

She drained her drink and called for the bill. "Honestly, I hired you to find Dylan. You failed. Now you're asking if I know of anyone else who'd kill Daddy dear?" She pushed back her chair. "If Dylan didn't do it, although I believe he did, I'm sure there is a slew of sleaze balls willing and able to take my father's money for their own. Now that Ben Pilkosky is dead, killed by that girl who worked for him, he's no help. Though personally, I think he was lining his pockets with my family's money. No doubt other people's money too." She stood and heaved her purse onto her shoulder. "Who knows? Maybe he was involved with that old-time gangster Tommy

Allegro worked for."

My martini sloshed in my belly. "Michael Bucanetti?"

"Whoever."

She turned her back to me and strolled out of the restaurant as if she had it all under control.

I, on the other hand, felt like one of those springy toys, bouncing up and down and around in absolutely no purposeful direction.

It was late, but I had to talk to somebody. Ed. Except I knew he hadn't been feeling well and so, decided I'd swallow my urge and go home for some sleep.

As if he'd read the energy I'd just put out, my phone rang. It was Ed. Dear, wonderful Ed. "Ed, it's late. You should be in bed."

He sneezed. "Eh, I'm all right. Besides, I been sleeping most of the day, except for a few calls I made to some people I know."

I was suddenly alert. "Do you have something for me?"

"You might say that. In fact, you might say I got a whole lot of something for you." He paused and cleared his throat. "I just heard back from a guy who knows a guy. Anyway, according to them, Pilkosky was in deep with the ponies and anything else he could bet on. Guess who owned the chits?"

"Tommy Allegro?"

His information not such a surprise, he sounded deflated. "Yeah." But his enthusiasm popped back quickly. "Bet you didn't know that Tommy unloaded them to none other than—"

With a groan, I interrupted. "Michael Bucanetti."

Ed huffed. "Right. Not sure why Bucanetti would take that on."

I chewed on the inside of my cheek. "Maybe to have some control over Pilkosky. I mean, maybe Pilkosky could help him get him some respectability? Force him to introduce Bucanetti to the right people."

"Don't think so. Bucanetti most likely already has his stubby fingers in all sorts of legit businesses."

"Yeah, you're probably right, which means I'll have to find out what's behind Bucanetti buying the chits. Not that I think he killed Pilkosky. Loan sharks don't kill the goose. They just break their wings if they don't pay. Hey Ed, thank you for following up on this, especially when you're sick."

"Hey, no *problemo*. Anyway, they say it's in sickness and in health…" He chuckled. "No, I guess that's for marriage." A cough, followed by a sneeze. "I'm gonna take some more of that nighttime stuff that knocks ya out, and I'll be good as new tomorrow."

"You do that, Ed. But if you still feel sick, you stay home. Promise?"

Grudgingly, he agreed. "You're as bad as Lena, always looking out for me."

I ended the call, then rubbed the sleepiness out of my eyes. I still had to do something to help Nadia, my former prison mate. Letting Harold, as her lawyer, know about Bucanetti's connection to Pilkosky could help establish a motive for why Pilkosky might have been embezzling money. I then began to think about how this new information affected my case, but the wheels in my mind couldn't turn. No gas. I needed some sleep. Maybe then, fresh, I'd start with why Pilkosky ended up owing Bucanetti and what that led to.

I trudged home, took care of Charlie, and hopped into bed for a few hours' respite.

Chapter Fifteen

THE NEXT MORNING my phone was ringing, but Charlie was lying on my arm. I gently nudged him and with a doggy groan, he rolled off and I grabbed my phone just before the call went into voicemail.

With a sleepy croak, I answered. It was Corrigan.

"Meet me at John's Diner in twenty minutes."

"What? Why?" I absently ran my free hand over my wrinkled 'I love chocolate' t-shirt.

"That's six thirty. I got Sarah Mueller." He ended the call.

I stared at the phone, ready to call him back. But Charlie was up and doing his 'I gotta go outside' dance. I groaned, grabbed his leash, threw a ratty sweater over my sleep attire and opened the door. "You've got to make this quick, Charlie."

He did, and I made it to John's Diner only one minute late.

Corrigan and the bags under his eyes from lack of sleep were already waiting for me. He was drinking a cup of coffee, and a diet pop sat waiting for me. I slid into the booth upholstered in fake leather.

Setting his coffee down, he glanced at his watch. "You made it and only one minute late." He yawned, a big, jaw-cracking one, spoiling whatever effect his comment was supposed to make.

"I'll admit it was a close one. Now tell me. How did you capture Sarah? What about Dylan?"

He took a gulp of his coffee. "I'll make it quick because I'm back on duty this morning. I'd questioned Sarah right after the murder and left my card. She called me last night. Claimed everything she did was because Dylan made her do it." He shrugged. "That's what they all say. Anyway, she said she snuck away while they were waiting at a bus stop."

My throat felt awfully dry so I took a sip of the icy pop. "Did she say where he's planning on going?"

He shook his head. "He didn't tell her, but he could be headed to Toledo then maybe Detroit or Chicago. We've still got an APB out on him, so he'll turn up."

Sinking into the tufted back of the booth, I asked, "Where is Sarah now?"

"At the station. And, no, you can't talk to her. This was a courtesy call, Claire."

Leaning across the table, I declared, "Dylan killed his father. This proves it."

Corrigan stretched and made a circle with his neck. I

noticed he'd missed a spot shaving. "Claire, it doesn't prove anything. Sarah's claiming Dylan was with her when Paul Morley died. And she's not budging on that."

I slammed my forearms on the slightly sticky table. "I don't believe her. None of it. First, she didn't seem unwilling to stick me in that closet."

"Yeah, well, who do you think called the cops to get you out?"

I sighed. "Okay, so she's not a bad guy and Dylan is. I won't press charges against her. Okay? Now, any hope of catching her boyfriend? Soon?"

He folded his arms across his chest. "We'll get him, and if he killed Morley, I'll find out."

Not wanting to argue this early in the morning, I nodded and kept any thoughts to myself.

Peering into my face, Corrigan smiled wistfully. "You know, even at this hour, you're pretty hot." Then, as if he'd said more than he'd intended, he cleared his throat, and threw down some dollar bills. "Gotta go. But, I'll be in touch."

He hustled from the booth as if he were a hunted man. I twisted my mouth and thought about it. In some ways, I guessed he was.

I took a final sip of my pop and then also left the diner, my mind swirling. Could Dylan really be his father's killer? I couldn't make that stick to him, but what about Janette? She certainly had a motive. I shook my head and drove home to shower and dress appropriately for the day ahead. Then I'd see if Ed was feeling well enough to help me dig into Paul's murkier connections.

ℰᏠℭ

ED AND I MUST HAVE been thinking the same thing because he called me just as I was getting out of the shower. "Hey kiddo. I'm feeling tip-top today. Must've had one of those twenty-four hour bugs. I'm thinking I could do some more digging into Morley's financial accomplices."

Throwing on some clothes, I responded, "I was hoping you'd say that. But only if you're really up to it."

"Are you kidding? I'm rarin' to go. Lena's been running home and feeding me as if I was a whole country. I gotta get out of here before I balloon into the size of one."

I chuckled. "Yeah, my aunt believes in feeding a cold *and* feeding a fever. Okay. See what you can find. In the meantime, I'm going back to where it all began. Lake Erie Yacht Club. I want to talk to the waitress who usually waited on Paul. I think her name is Brenda and it seemed like they had a special friendship or whatever. Maybe she knows something the cops missed. Some clue. I don't know, but I have to do *some*thing." I sighed trying to convince myself this wouldn't be a waste of time.

"Ed didn't respond for a second, then said, "Hope you find what you need." By his tone, I don't think he believed I would. "You sure they'll let you in?"

I huffed. "I'll find a way."

It didn't take a lot of time to get to the yacht club, but getting inside was a different story. Without a member's pass it was nearly impossible to get beyond the elderly guard. His white hair and beard made me think of a kindly gentleman who, during the Christmas season, would pad himself and work in department stores. Too bad there was no *ho, ho, ho* when I asked him if I could park in the lot.

"I'm sorry miss, but no pass, no parking."

"Not even in the visitor's lot? Please. It's important! I have business here."

He pulled out a clipboard. "Name?"

"Claire DeNardo."

"Ho! You're the one who killed Mr. Morley."

"Allegedly. And I didn't do it. Honest." I opened my eyes wide and gave him a smile so innocent-looking I could have been beamed up to heaven that instant. "Please."

He grumbled. "Who do you want to see?"

Hope sprang in my chest. "Someone who works in the restaurant, a server." The expression on my face probably looked like Charlie's when he wants a walk and a chew toy.

The guard scowled. "Okay, but you have to park over there." He pointed to a tiny dirt area.

"Thank you. So much."

He mumbled something I wasn't sure I wanted to hear.

I parked and dodged around the puddles and tire ruts. Difficult though it was, I ignored the police tape surrounding Paul's boat and entered the Lake Erie Yacht Club's restaurant.

All did not go smoothly. First, the maître d', the same

man who greeted Paul and me stopped me. His head jerked back. "What are you doing here? Get out."

My face felt hot enough to melt chocolate. This was the man who saw me covered in blood and testified to that. I stood my ground but my voice shook. "I'll only be a minute. Please. Let me talk to Brenda."

"She's busy with customers."

I glanced around. He and I were the only ones in the restaurant except for one guy sitting alone at the bar.

I folded my hands as if in prayer. "It won't take long, I promise. Then I'll leave."

He crossed his arms and harrumphed, "Anyway, why? The cops didn't need to talk to her."

"They already thought they had a case against me." I looked at him as if to say, "And you're responsible, telling them I was covered in blood."

He must have gotten my meaning. "I shouldn't let you, but…okay, but if you cause any trouble, I'm calling the police." He spun on his heels, giving me no clue whether to follow him or not. So, I stayed put.

A minute later, a gorgeous young woman with porcelain skin and thick chestnut-colored hair tied back exited the kitchen and headed towards me. "I'm Brenda. You wanted to talk to me?"

Her tone was anything but friendly. Still, I seized my chance. "Paul Morley had nothing but praise for you. As if, maybe you were closer than server and client? I was hoping you could tell me anything that might help me find out who killed him and why."

She leaned back, hands on her hips. "Only thing I know is he was a generous tipper, and I don't think anyone dies from that." She turned to walk away, but I grabbed her arm. "Any reason you weren't working that morning?"

Her jaw was clenched, and she glared at me. Finally, she spit out, "The new waitress, Mandy, had an emergency and needed to switch shifts. I took her Sunday evening shift." She shrugged, "Better tips anyway. I have to go."

"Wait. One more second. Mandy's last name?" I wondered if the cops had talked to Mandy or had just skipped that part of the investigation, figuring I was the obvious killer.

"Williams." She pulled away from me and strode back into the kitchen.

The maître d' lost no time in hustling toward me, menace on his face. "Okay. You talked to her. Now, go or I call the cops."

I headed toward the restaurant's exit with him following closely. Over my shoulder, I asked, "When does Mandy come in?"

The maître d' huffed. "She quit, and you're done. Get out. Now."

I was backing out the door asking for her address, but got no answer that could be repeated in polite company. I needed to find Mandy Williams. Maybe she knew something, or saw something and then, frightened, made herself scarce.

‘’‘

IT SEEMED LIKE AN ETERNITY since I'd been at my office to work, but everything still looked fine. Except for the cup of what had been tea but now was growing something that looked like it came from a swamp. Maybe I needed to invest in finding a new assistant who would mind the place. I'd already been through two. Of course, who would take a job now with an employer charged with murder?

I checked messages on my office phone first. There was only one, and that was about buying an extended warrantee on my car. I pursed my lips, making a mental note to do more advertising as soon as I was cleared of Paul's murder. Assuming that glorious day ever came.

I powered up my computer and started digging for information on Mandy Williams. I wondered if that was really her name.

An hour later, I'd gotten a lead on two different women with that name. One was in her eighties, but the other seemed about the right age, twenty-three.

Last known address was a hotel in Mayfield Heights, on Cleveland's East Side. My brow knitted. That was a long way to come to work at Lake Erie Yacht Club on the West Side.

I shrugged and called the listed phone number. A man answered, "Blidden House. Can I help you?"

Scrunching up my face, I asked, "Is Mandy Williams there?"

"I'm sorry. I can't give out the names of our residents."

"Residents? What kind of place is this?"

He cleared his throat. "We're a small boutique hotel. If you're interested, I can give you our website—"

"No, no. That's fine. Has this always been your phone number?"

"Yes, of course."

"Can I leave a message for Mandy Williams?"

"Her suite number, please?"

I growled softly. "Never mind. Thank you." I ended the call, deciding I'd visit the place, but first, I called Harold to tell him about Pilkosky's nasty gambling habit and his connection to Bucanetti.

It went into voicemail. "Harold, it's Claire. Call me back. On second thought, no need. Just wanted to tell you—"

Harold's voice cut me off. "Claire! You are the very person I wished to speak with!"

The hairs on my arms stood up. I suspected Harold was plotting something that I wouldn't like. "What did you want to tell me, Harold?"

"Another of my clients, the person you referred, believes she knows why Mr. Pilkosky, the deceased, may have stolen funds."

I pressed my lips together. "Why?"

"She believes he owed money to somebody who would hurt him if he didn't pay it back." He lowered his voice. "I believe this all may be linked to a person with whom we've had recent dealings."

I wanted to scream at him, but managed to keep calm.

"Are we talking about Michael Bucanetti?"

His voice went up an octave. "What? No, of course not! Why would you say that?"

I closed my eyes and silently prayed for patience. "Pilkosky owed Bucanetti a lot of money because of gambling debts. Who were you talking about?"

"My client and I thought Mr. Pilkosky was indebted to Paul Morley."

"Hmm. There may be something to that. I think these two murders are probably linked. But I just don't have all the pieces. Unless…"

"Unless what, my dear lady?"

Right now I only wanted him to know that Bucanetti held the chits on Pilkosky. I couldn't have Harold blundering along with a half-baked theory of motive until I knew all the facts. "Unless somebody else had it in for Pilkosky. Remember, I heard him arguing with a woman just before he died. Anyway, just know that Pilkosky owed Bucanetti big time. Maybe he was scared enough to embezzle money to pay off his debts."

"Oh. I see. And, this knowledge could help my other client with the original charge of embezzlement by pointing the finger at Mr. Pilkosky."

"Exactly." *How had he ever been allowed to be an attorney?* "Okay, Harold, I have to go. Let me know if you uncover anything that'll help my case. Remember, I'm your client too."

"Of course. I shall not forget that."

I ended the call, frustrated. But at least I'd provided a

clue that could help Nadia.

My good deed done, I made one more call, this time to Ed. I hoped that if I needed some muscle to persuade the guy at Blidden House's front desk to let me talk to Mandy, Ed could fill the bill.

"Hey, kiddo. Whatcha need?" I made my request, but it wasn't to be. "Sorry. No can do. I'm about to meet with a guy who claims he knows where some of Morley's skeletons are buried."

"That's okay, Ed. I'll just charm the guy with my intense good looks." I chuckled, not feeling the humor.

Flying solo, I headed out to Blidden House carrying a somewhat dated picture of Mandy Williams. It was a long drive, but I hoped it'd be worth it.

ഇൽ

HIGHWAY TRAFFIC wasn't as bad as I'd expected, and I arrived at Blidden House in less than forty minutes. The place looked pretty fancy from the outside, like a boutique hotel, but maybe it had long term guests too.

Walking through the grand entrance, I wondered how a waitress could afford a place like this. A carved mahogany desk situated in a gold-rimmed alcove sat across from the entrance way. A young man was sorting papers there.

I approached him, "Excuse me, have you seen this woman?" I held up Mandy's picture.

He pushed his glasses up on his nose and stood. "Who

wants to know?"

I decided to make it sound official. "I'm a private investigator, looking into a crime that she may have some information about. Now, is she here or not?"

He curled his upper lip. "I don't have to do anything you say. You're not a real cop."

Behind me, a male voice boomed, "But I am." It was Corrigan and his badge.

I spun around. "Why are you here?"

"Later." He addressed the clerk again. "Are you going to let us talk to Mandy Williams now?"

The clerk cleared his throat and checked his nearby computer. "Um, I'm sorry detective. Ms. Williams checked out yesterday. No forwarding address."

Butting in, I asked, "How long did she live here, and did she say where she came from?"

Glancing from me to Corrigan, the clerk answered, "She stayed here for three weeks, and all I know is, she said she was from Chicago."

Seemed pretty suspicious to me and apparently to Corrigan too because his next question was, "Did she mention anything about her job? If not to you, did she associate with anybody else here?"

The clerk's Adam's apple bounced in his skinny neck. "No sir. Nothing to me and I never saw her with anyone else."

I was the first to accept this was a dead end. "Thank you for your help."

Corrigan joined in. "Yeah, thanks."

It wasn't until we were both outside the place that I started badgering Corrigan. "Now will you tell me why you're here?"

He kept walking. "Ed called me and told me what you were up to. He was worried, so I offered to swing by."

"Just like that?" I snapped my fingers. "You just dropped everything to help me?" We were approaching his car and, to my discomfort, I spotted the always ravishing Abby, waiting patiently in the passenger seat.

My hand automatically went to my hair, which I recalled I hadn't even combed after my shower.

No doubt she was subtracting attractiveness points from me. I'm sure she also noticed that the hem on my skirt was drooping on one side. Abby lowered her window. "Hello, Claire."

I tried to sound casual. "Hi. How are you?"

I didn't have to listen to her reply because my phone rang. "Hello, Ed."

"Hey, kiddo. Don't get all twisted. I sent Brian there to make sure you were okay."

Corrigan and Abby were both watching me, so I smiled but it was as phony as a rubber snake. "Oh, you thought a hotel clerk could take me down?"

He quickly protested. "No. You're tough as they come, Claire. I found out that place doesn't exactly do background checks on their residents. Some pretty rough people have stayed there. I didn't want anything bad happening."

My first impulse was to ask him for details, but I didn't

want to air my business in front of Corrigan and especially Abby. "How about we meet at my office in an hour? You can tell me everything then."

"Sure, boss."

I ended the call and found that both Corrigan and Abby were still keeping their eyes on me. I could tell he was getting ready to lecture me, but I couldn't read what she was thinking. She was probably noticing all my flaws.

To throw Corrigan and Abby off, I decided to be gracious. "I appreciate both of you for coming down here to make sure I was all right."

Abby merely nodded, but Corrigan's one eyebrow rose. "Yeah? You have a funny way of showing your appreciation, DeNardo." He opened his car door and turned back to me. "Mind if I have that picture of Mandy Williams? I'll see if I can find where she disappeared to."

I hated to admit how defeated I felt. I couldn't exactly cry on his shoulder that things weren't working out. Big girls don't do that, and I was a big girl. Instead, I sighed and shrugged my shoulders. " Well, it was really a long shot coming here." Handing him the picture, I said, "I'd appreciate knowing anything you find out about her." Corrigan's eyes searched my face. "If anything comes up, you know I'll be there." With that, he drove away and I stood there feeling empty. I chalked it up to a wasted trip to Blidden House.

I got back into my car while questions about how Mandy afforded this place and why she disappeared so quickly after Paul's death stayed in my mind the whole way back to my office.

In fact, I posed them to Ed the minute I got through my office door.

Ed played with his coffee stirrer. "I might have an answer for you. The guy I talked to while you were at Blidden House didn't come through with what I'd hoped. But he did have some info that's mighty handy."

"What?"

He smirked. "Bucanetti."

I puckered my lips and shook my head. "What does he have to do with anything today?"

He pitched the coffee stirrer. "Guess who owns Blidden House?"

I went cold inside. "Bucanetti?"

"Well, not outright. According to this guy, a company called HappyHomes owns it. But three guesses who's behind that cheerful name?"

I felt like shrinking and crawling inside my desk drawer. "That's why you called Corrigan?"

"Yep. Given your history with that mobster, I didn't want to take any chances you'd get hurt."

My eyes opened wide. "If Bucanetti ultimately owns Blidden House, there's probably a connection between him and Mandy Williams. I don't know what it is yet, but I'd bet a whole tray of chocolate chip brownies it centers around Paul Morley." That started me thinking about who I might need to visit next. And I felt as solid as a boiled too long piece of linguine.

Chapter Sixteen

I KNEW BEFORE I SAID IT out loud that Ed would argue with me. And he did. "Kiddo, we don't know if it was a coincidence or not. No sense crawling into the lion's den before you know if he's just eaten. Speaking of eating, I stopped to let Lena know I was okay and she gave me these." He opened an oil-stained bag that smelled of chocolate. *Tricolore* cookies, covered in chocolate with strawberry jam between the red and green layers.

I grabbed one, thinking how easy it would be to talk me out of confronting Michael Bucanetti. He and I had made an uneasy peace with each other a while ago, but before that, it had felt as if my life had an early expiration date. In fact, my whole family had targets on their backs. "You're right. I need to think carefully about my next step here. What else did your informant tell you?"

"Not much, beside about Blidden House's ownership. He did tell me, though, that Morley invested heavy with

Pilkosky's firm. According to my guy, they shared something else. Pilkosky introduced Morley to none other than Bucanetti and that Bucanetti had hired Morley to handle some negotiations."

My interest piqued. "With who? For what?"

Ed blew out a deep breath. "He didn't know the particulars. Or, if he did, he was too keen on living to tell me."

I finished a second cookie and fought against taking a third. "Okay, so we know Paul and Bucanetti had some sort of dealings. We also know the waitress he and I had the day he died was staying at a place owned by Bucanetti." I paused for effect. "Looks like all roads lead to him."

"Sure does." Ed went into the kitchen to make some more coffee when my phone rang. It was Corrigan, sounding a bit out of breath. "Claire, I don't have long to talk but I got some more details on that waitress. Her real name is Eileen Murphy. She's originally from Chicago but she travels. A lot. She's believed to be responsible for the deaths of four people, maybe more. But no charges have ever stuck. Word is she's done at least one of those killings for Michael Bucanetti. Bad news is we don't have her in custody yet."

I winced, as if Corrigan had stuck me with a voodoo pin. That meant I'd have to confront the gangster, something I did not want. Our agreement had been to keep out of each other's way. Confronting him could mean walking into his deadly web again. I felt nauseated.

"Claire? You're awfully quiet. I know what's going on in that sharp little mind of yours. Don't do it. Stay away from Bucanetti. You could be risking your life for nothing we can use in court. His word against yours. And don't forget, a condition of your parole is to not associate with known felons and Bucanetti is one of the best known ones."

I faked surprise. "I wouldn't even think of going to see him. He's almost killed me a few times already." Despite my words, I knew I had no choice. This was my life and my freedom at stake. If Bucanetti was the key to proving my innocence I had to do whatever it took to bring him in. Even at gun point. My muscles tensed just thinking about it.

Corrigan's next words broke into my thoughts. "You're still going to see him, aren't you?" His voice turned pensive. "You know, there may be another way to get to him."

My heart began beating harder. If I didn't have to confront Bucanetti it would continue beating for a long time. "How?"

"We just keep looking for Eileen and get her to confess."

My excitement evaporated, replaced by my old friend, hopelessness. "And if you either don't find her or she doesn't confess, then what?"

He didn't say anything, but I heard him loud and clear.

"That's what I thought. Somehow, I've got to get an admission of guilt you can use."

"Are you sure you want to do this? Confront Bucanetti?"

I grimaced and put as much steel into my voice as I could manage. "Yes."

He sounded as if I'd knocked the wind out of him. "Okay, okay. Come down to the station and we'll talk."

My stomach churned. The two cookies I'd consumed suddenly felt as heavy as a tombstone. "I'll be down there in fifteen minutes."

I gave Ed a short explanation, including the waitress's real identity and that murder seemed to be her chosen career path. I was rewarded with a disapproving look from him. "I hope Brian can talk you out of this cockeyed plan."

I ignored his comment, grabbed my purse and took off, making it to the police station in twelve minutes.

Corrigan was on the phone, but Abby was waiting for me. "Well, well, what do you know? I haven't seen you in months, but now today I've already seen you twice."

Her sarcastic tone did nothing to ease my skittishness. Knowing I had no witty answer, I opted for "Hello, Abby."

"We'll go into Interrogation Room Three. When Brian gets off the phone, he'll fill you in."

I followed her, my head held high. At least I could pretend I had confidence. We sat across from each other waiting. I played with the strap on my purse. Every minute seemed to last an hour.

Abby adjusted the clip she'd used to hold back her luxurious hair and cleared her throat. "I just want to say something before Brian comes in."

I stiffened, waiting for some new insult. Instead her voice softened. "Brian and I don't work. I mean, we're great as work partners, but not romantically." She chortled. "What I'm trying to say is he's yours. I don't get it, but behind those blue eyes is nothing but feelings for you." She shrugged, as if trying to get a nasty bug off her shoulder. "Anyway, I needed to say that. Not that you deserve it, but he's still got an unshakeable thing for you."

All of a sudden, I felt dizzy, unable to think of anything to say that would make a bit of sense. With great effort, I managed a weak, "Oh!"

The door opened and Corrigan walked in, looking first at me and then at Abby. "What's going on?"

Abby shrugged. "Oh, nothing. We were just making small talk, weren't we, Claire?"

"Yeah, nothing important." My hand fluttered to my throat like those Victorian ladies that always seemed ready to faint.

Corrigan looked as if he was going to ask another question, but chose to just scowl. He turned a chair backwards and sat down. "Okay, Claire, here's the deal. I'd still rather find Eileen, and I want you to give me twenty-four hours to do that. If we can't track her down, we'll go to Plan B."

My body went through another change. Now I felt clammy and I rubbed my hands together to create warmth. "I go see Bucanetti."

That tiny vein in his forehead pulsed. "Yeah, but you'll be wearing a wire."

My rear almost lifted out of the chair. "What? What if he spots it?"

"He won't. You ask to meet in a public place. We'll be nearby monitoring everything that goes down." He leaned in toward me, hands gripping his chair tight. "I'll make sure nothing happens to you. I swear."

A millisecond passed and I realized Corrigan was right. I'd be a fool to think Bucanetti would confess and let me bring him in. I inhaled deeply. "Okay, first you get until six p.m. tomorrow to find Eileen." I'd pray extra hard he would. "If not, I go after Bucanetti." I was putting up a brave front, but my insides felt as if they had been placed in a blender.

We established a time when I'd hear one way or the other. I then revealed how I'd call on Tommy Allegro. Convince him I had some information about Eileen that Bucanetti would want and have Tommy set a meet-up between Bucanetti and me.

Abby's nose wrinkled. "Why bother with Allegro? That guy's scum."

"Yes, I know, but he's easier to reach than Bucanetti. I mean, I doubt anyone just drops in to see the top guy. I've already talked to Allegro once and he didn't hurt me. Besides, it's not like I know where Bucanetti is. I don't have a tracker on him."

Corrigan frowned. "I don't like it, but you've got a point."

A few tweaks later the plan was settled, and Corrigan walked me to my car. "We'll get Eileen, I'm sure of it."

Though I silently gave him credit for his bravado, my fears remained.

I turned to him. "I know you're doing everything you can."

I drove away, ironically feeling as if I'd been comforting him.

By the time I reached my office, I'd convinced myself Eileen was just around the corner, waiting to be caught and to confess. Then once I was free, I could concentrate on what Abby had told me. To be truthful, though, our conversation wove its way through all my other thoughts.

Back at my office, Ed brought me back to reality. "What did Brian cook up to catch this killer waitress?"

I explained the plan. He shook his head harder with each sentence. "Those wires don't always work the way they do on television. If they can't find the lady, why don't I go see Bucanetti instead?"

A wave of warm gratitude passed through me and I wanted to hug him. But I couldn't let him risk his life. This was my mess to clean up, unfortunately.

ॐं

ED AND I FELL INTO our usual pattern of working. He made calls to anybody he knew who might have information about the relationship between Paul and Bucanetti. To both our frustration, he came up empty.

Meanwhile I did everything I could think of, including calling Lake Erie Yacht Club and pestering them about their former employee. Nothing.

Hours later, my stomach growled and I had a stiff neck. I stretched and turned to Ed. "I hope the cops got further looking for Eileen."

I glanced at the clock just as my phone rang. "Claire, is my husband there?"

"Yes, he's here." I silently mouthed Aunt Lena's name to Ed. "He's just on his way out."

She huffed. "He better be. You know, he's just recovering from what could've been a serious illness. And he's not getting any younger. He shouldn't work so hard." She chortled. "Look who I'm telling that to. I bet you haven't even eaten yet. You'll run yourself down. You're getting too skinny. Men may say they want a skinny woman, but they really don't. In fact—"

"Aunt Lena, Ed should be home soon and I'm also leaving. I'll have a big dinner. Okay?"

She sniffed. "Big dinner. Sure. Probably one of those frozen things. You know, you're always welcome to come over."

I loved my aunt, but I didn't have it in me to spar with her that evening. "I appreciate it, but I have to take care of Charlie and I really want to relax at my place."

"Just make sure you eat properly. I love you."

"Love you too."

Ed was putting his cap on just as the call ended. "You know what a great cook your aunt is. And she always makes enough for an army. Come on over."

"No. I appreciate it, but I really want to just chill. I'll

call you tomorrow. Thanks Ed. For everything."

He saluted me. "Happy to work for ya." With that he left me alone in my office.

I was closing up shop when my conversation with Abby intruded once again into my thoughts. I blew out a breath. Maybe I wouldn't be able to wait until I was a free woman to decide what I really felt. But right now, I was tired and hungry. I yawned and turned out the office lights.

୫

CHARLIE WAS HAPPY to see me, as always. If only Bucanetti would be as happy, but that was a pipedream. I shivered just thinking about encountering him again. He looked like somebody's kindly grandpa with his protruding belly and gray hair, but his soul was part snake and the other part shark.

Charlie must have sensed my unease, because he yipped and snuggled up to me as if to assure me of his protection. My dog, my bodyguard. I sighed wistfully and rubbed his head hard.

We took a walk and I talked as he sniffed the area around my apartment building. "Charlie, after we get done with this murder investigation, what would you think about Corrigan coming around more often?"

He wagged his tail and barked, as if he'd understood me. Maybe he understood a lot more than I did.

Back inside, I fed my pup first, then looked in my refrigerator and sighed. Nothing there except diet pop and a shriveled tomato. My freezer didn't hold much promise, either. One frozen dinner covered with ice. It'd have to do. I dug further into the freezer and uncovered a foil wrapped chocolate cupcake. At least I'd have dessert.

My dinner heating up in the microwave, I flicked on the television. There wasn't much on so I turned to an old movie, the black-and-white kind. A frothy romance. I hoped it was enough to give my overworked brain a respite.

Once Charlie and I finished our separate meals, he snuggled up to me and we fell asleep. So tired, I don't think I even dreamt.

On the other hand, Charlie must have had hunting dreams that following morning because his short legs were moving, waking me up. A look at the clock told me it was five in the morning. I gently extricated myself from my dog and stretched. My stomach complained loudly. I guess it felt cheated with the skimpy and somewhat freezer-burned meal it'd had the previous night.

I stumbled into the shower, brushed my teeth and dressed. My furry companion was up and ready for his morning stroll. By the time we'd completed that and he'd eaten, I was starving. I don't work very well on a totally empty stomach, so I needed to stop for something to eat. Breadly's was on the way to my office, so I planned on driving there for a chocolate chip scone. Maybe two. I'd lost weight since I'd been incarcerated, so I didn't feel guilty.

I pulled up to Breadly's drive-thru and placed my

order. Thoughts of Corrigan and of Bucanetti vied for uppermost spot in my head. I squashed both of them down mercilessly. "Later." I told my brain. I rubbed my face, feeling wrung out already.

The first thing I did at the office was to turn on my computer. Then I checked the time. Corrigan now had only eleven hours to hunt down Eileen. I pulled the scone from the bag, but all of a sudden it didn't look as appetizing.

I was struggling to get it down my tightened throat when Ed strolled in holding a casserole dish covered with foil. "Hey kiddo. Lena insisted I bring you this. It's chicken cacciatore. I'll put it in the fridge in case you get hungry later."

"Thanks, Ed." If a giant meteor stuck the earth, Aunt Lena would make sure everyone ate before being annihilated.

Ed got himself a cup of coffee and pulled a chair up next to me. "You give any more thought to that crazy scheme of yours?"

My mouth full of scone, I shook my head. "I'm trying not to, until I know for sure I have to."

He nodded, then stretched his arms out and interlaced his fingers, as if readying to play a piano. "Got a few more people I can call. Maybe we'll catch a break."

I gave him a half-hearted smile. "Yeah, maybe."

Chapter Seventeen

ED AND I GOT NOWHERE, and I was about to call it quits when Corrigan called. My heart stopped beating for a second.

"Claire, um, we found Eileen Murphy." From his hesitant tone, I could tell there was something else and it wouldn't be good. "She was in Cincinnati."

I couldn't wait any longer. "And? Has she confessed?"

He blew out a deep breath. "She's unconscious. The Cincinnati cops believe she was in the process of completing another hit. It went sideways and now she's in the hospital with a bullet wound to her head. Of course, we're keeping it under wraps."

Any light at the end of the tunnel I imagined faded and disappeared. My throat constricted, but the words needed to come out. "So that means I go see Bucanetti."

Trying to inject some hope into this situation he added, "She's under guard and could wake up any minute."

"I can't wait for 'any minute'. I'll find Tommy Allegro and through him, Bucanetti."

"Claire, wait! You can't—"

"You're right. I can't just wait around. I'll let you know when my meeting with Bucanetti is set."

I ended the call, feeling Ed's eyes on me. I put up my hands. "Please don't say anything. I've got to do this."

Ed shook his head. "Okay, but I can at least go with you to visit Allegro. Make sure he keeps those sleazy hands of his from roaming across your body."

I cringed and clutched my blouse remembering my last encounter with that worm. "I think that's a very good idea."

"What're you planning on giving Allegro for his help?"

My mind went blank. How could I let that slip? Of course he'd want something in return. I just didn't know what. "I'll offer him money. Do you think he'll take a post-dated check?"

Ed chuckled, as if I was kidding. "I'll cover it for you. I'd rather that than him wanting his payment in flesh."

"Ugh. Seriously, though. I can't let you do that. I already owe my freedom to my father and your wife."

He grabbed my arms. "It ain't nothing but money, kiddo."

I reluctantly agreed, but in the back of my mind I searched for a different way of paying Allegro.

I thought about what I would say to the petty criminal. It had to be good enough that he'd persuade Bucanetti to see me. I didn't like it, but I felt comfortable enough fabricating a story about Eileen Murphy to spur him into action.

I had it down pat. I took a shaky breath. "Let's get this over with, Ed."

He nodded and we headed to my car in silence.

The trip to Fun Times, Tommy Allegro's bowling emporium and office, seemed to take less than a minute. Of course, my foot was pressed pretty hard on the gas.

I silently ran through my spiel, nodded at Ed, and got out of the car. I fidgeted with my hair all the way into the bowling emporium. I whispered out of the side of my mouth, "Let's hope Allegro's here."

Ed squeezed the top of my arm. "This'll go as smooth as cream cheese."

We nonchalantly made it to the back of the huge building and as before, ran into Allegro's massive body guard, Maurice. My breath grew a bit more ragged realizing that this was it. Allegro would be in his office.

Before I could press the Up button for the elevator, Maurice grabbed my hand and squeezed it hard. "Nobody goes upstairs without permission."

I sprung into my role as temptress. Batting my lashes and sticking out my chest, I purred, "Don't you remember me? Tommy and I planned a little, you know, fun time." I placed my free hand on Maurice's stone hard chest. "You understand."

He looked from me to Ed and back again, releasing my hand. "Don't move. I'm calling Mr. Allegro."

He whispered into his phone while my heart pounded.

"Okay, he says you can go up, but Grandpa here has to stay with me."

Ed's fists clenched, either because he wanted to protect me or he took exception to being called grandpa.

I winked at Maurice. "That's fine. I won't be too long." The elevator doors closed and I lowered my head to halt my lightheadedness.

I walked down to Allegro's office, feeling as if I was walking the final mile. He was sitting behind his desk, hands behind his head, relaxed.

"Couldn't get enough of the Tommy charm, huh?" He chuckled and then motioned to a chair. "Have a seat, honey. What's up?"

Don't lose your cool now. "I need to speak to Michael Bucanetti. Get me a meeting."

He pulled out a cigarette and lit it. "Sure, you got that nosy detective off my scent. But why should I set anything up for you?"

I swallowed. "I know who killed Paul Morley and I can prove it. Right now, the cops are following up on other persons of interest, maybe even including you. But I don't want to go to the cops with my proof. At least, not before I talk to Mr. Bucanetti. In a public place. And then, we'll see."

Allegro looked me up and down, like an alligator wondering if I'd be a worthwhile meal. "What's in it for me? I mean, I'd be sticking my neck out. I need more than your pretty face showing gratitude."

"Meaning what?" I ignored my racing pulse.

"You're gonna ask Bucanetti for money, aren't you?"

"And if I am?"

He shrugged, "I'm not greedy. How about ten grand? Up front."

I stifled a nervous laugh. "Ten thousand what? Kisses? Hugs?"

He pounded his desk so hard I almost jumped. "I'm not kidding. Either you agree to my price, or get the hell out of here."

Summoning my failing nerve I blurted, "What about five thousand? And the money after you set the meeting up."

"Seven. And I'll throw in that extra time to pay me." He chuckled meanly. "Take it. It's a bargain."

I made a quick calculation in my mind. If I sold my car, and borrowed a bit more, I could pay that and not use so much of Ed's money. "Okay. Once the meeting is set up, I'll arrange to pay you." I laid my business card on his desk.

He smiled, but it didn't reach his eyes. "I'm glad we could do business. I'll call you with the details." He stood and walked around his desk. "Good to see you again."

I stood too, but I think my stomach was still in the chair. My legs felt wooden but I made it out of his office and into the hallway. The elevator went down and took my spirits with it. I was surely descending into Hell.

Ed and I walked out of Fun Times in silence. In fact, I couldn't find my voice until we got inside my car.

Ed turned to me. "Okay, spill it. What happened?"

I cleared my throat. "It worked. Allegro's going to set up the meeting." I ran my hand over the steering wheel, wondering how fast I could sell my car.

"How much?"

"What? What do you mean?'

He spoke as if I had a hearing problem. "How much does he want to do this and when?"

I couldn't look him in the eye. "Seven thousand. To be paid once he gets the meeting in place." I quickly added, "But I can sell my car and maybe scrounge up the rest. I hate to take your money."

He sighed, "Kiddo, you need your car. Don't sell it. As for what you owe Allegro, leave it to me. Please."

My wall of resolve collapsed, and tears of gratitude and helplessness sprang to my eyes. "Ed I swear I'll pay you back. You, my dad, and Aunt Lena." I didn't have the slightest clue how I'd do that from prison. Maybe making lots of state license plates.

Chapter Eighteen

THE REST OF THE DAY I spent checking the clock. I hoped Allegro would call me soon, but maybe Bucanetti wasn't easy to get hold of. Or, maybe I was low priority on Allegro's list. In any case, I currently wasn't productive at all.

I did handle three phone calls, though. The first was Harold calling me. "Claire, this is Harold Goldfarb, your attorney."

I snapped, "Yes, I know who you are!" I instantly felt guilty for my impatience. "Sorry I snapped. What is it, Harold?" I said as sweetly as I could.

He cleared his throat, rather indignantly. Nonetheless, he continued. "I'd like to meet with you this Friday to discuss what we'll present in your defense."

My stomach twisted. If I couldn't get Bucanetti to admit he hired Eileen to kill Paul soon, my life as a free woman would end. I'd never even get the chance to consider what Abby told me about Corrigan. Or have a successful private detective agency run by me, an ace P.I.

Of course, when I first started out, I was afraid of everything, balloons and men's hairpieces, even chicken. I'd gotten past that and, though, a lot still frightened me, nothing came close to terrifying me as much as being imprisoned for a crime I didn't commit.

"Sure. What time and where, Harold?"

"My office, ten in the morning. And Claire, I will do everything in my power to get an acquittal for you."

I thanked him for his support though I believed unless he was a miracle worker it might be beyond his skill level. Then, just as we were ending the call, I decided to give him some hope for his other client, Nadia. "Harold, tell Nadia I might be able to shed some light on Pilkosky's murder."

"How? What are you going to do?"

I realized I'd said too much already. Aside from those who currently were in-the-know, nobody else should be informed about my meeting with Bucanetti. "Never mind. I'll let you know if it pans out." I ended the call before he could interrogate me further.

I silently sent up a prayer to Saint Jude Thaddeus, saint of impossible causes, to get that acquittal Harold talked about. Five minutes later, my phone went off again.

This time it was Corrigan. "How did it go with Tommy Allegro?" I gave him the current status update. He huffed, "Good work. But, um, you're not going to pay him."

My spine straightened. "But I have to. I have to get the

meeting."

"Claire, I'll take care of it. Just leave it to me. Allegro's going to get an offer he can't refuse. That is, if he wants to stay out of prison. Now, you've got enough to think about. Call me when the meeting is set."

Tired of putting up a strong front, I didn't argue. It was a relief to allow my load to lighten. "Thanks."

"It's okay. I also have some other news. We found Dylan Morley. Detroit police arrested him for trespassing and saw the APB we put out. They just notified us."

"So, that's good, isn't it?" I hoped so. I could definitely use any good news.

Corrigan hesitated for a moment. Then he added, "Yeah, it is."

Neither of us had much else to say, but plenty to think about. We cut the call short. It was just as well, since I then got the call I'd been waiting for. Tommy Allegro.

"It's set. Tonight at seven. Corsi's Italian Restaurant on Murray Hill."

I felt as if I was being choked. I began to see imaginary black swirls. I couldn't possibly be ready by tonight. "So soon?"

"Yeah. He says if you really got something, he wants to know about it pronto. He'll be waiting for you. And I'll be waiting for the seven thousand. I expect it by five today. If I don't get it, the meeting's off."

Trying not to think about the ramifications if Corrigan's plan for Tommy didn't work out, I faked a sureness I didn't feel. "Yes. Of course." The second the call ended, my mind switched to getting wired up and ready to confront the scariest person I knew. That, and of course, getting hold of Corrigan to set everything up.

Luckily, I reached Corrigan right away and told him about the meeting plans between Bucanetti and me. While my voice reached heights only dogs can hear, he stayed calm.

"We'll make sure Allegro gets what's coming to him. He won't suspect a thing. You'll need to come in to the station at four so we can get you set up to see Bucanetti."

Panic took up residence in me. "Are you positive you can get me ready and have everything in place on such short notice?"

"It'll be fine, Claire. I'll make sure of it."

I blew out a deep breath and it helped calm me. "Yeah, you're right. It'll go well." The call ended, as did any tranquility I'd managed to grab on to.

Ed, who'd been listening intently to my side of the call, prompted me. "Okay, so what did Brian tell you to do? He's going with you, isn't he? You can't go solo to meet Bucanetti at..."

Absently, I completed his sentence. "At Corsi's Italian." Realizing he'd gotten the name of the meet up, I held up my hand. "Never mind where. Anyway, it's all okay, Ed. Allegro will be paid, and I'm going to the police station at four. Brian insists everything will be set up and ready to go."

Ed twisted his mouth, as if to say he didn't believe any of it.

"I've got a few hours before I have to meet Corrigan, and there's a few things I need to take care of first. Hold down the fort, okay?"

"Sure. But can I do anything?"

I smiled and sadly shook my head. Then I left and headed home to Charlie, my loves-me-no-matter-what dog. First,

I planned to take him for a long walk, and then feed him. Give him a belly scratch and maybe even some peanut butter treats. He'd like that.

෨෬

OF COURSE, CHARLIE always delights in seeing me. This time was no different. We took a walk and then I fed him, even surprising him with some of the treats he loves. We played and I gave him hugs while he gave me doggy kisses. Finally, sadly, it was time for me to say goodbye. I closed the apartment door behind me, promising Charlie I'd try my hardest to come back alive.

Next was going to see my dad. I figured he deserved some of the time I had left. Unlike Charlie, though, my dad doesn't usually lay around waiting to see me. In fact, that afternoon he wasn't waiting. Suzy answered my knock on the door. "Claire, is something wrong?"

"No. I just wanted to see my dad again." I kept my voice low key and even. I certainly didn't want to worry anyone. I was toting enough worry for the whole Cleveland area.

"Oh, sorry. He's been feeling so bad about getting older and having no one young around, I sent him to the animal rescue center." She shrugged. "He could bring home a kitten and spoil it. Is there anything I can do?"

I cared for Suzy. She made my dad very happy and she'd been like a big sister to me. I hesitated, then shook my head. "It's nothing. Just tell him I love him. And you. A lot."

She squinted at me. "Okaay. Are you sure nothing's wrong?"

Even to me, my brightness felt phony. "No, nothing." I couldn't meet her eyes. "It's just that I miss him sometimes."

She gave me an unconvinced smile. "He misses you too. You know how much he loves you. As do I."

I smiled. "Thanks. That means a lot."

"Shall I have him call you?"

"No. I probably won't be available." *Or alive.* I practically bolted from the doorstep before Suzy could ask more questions.

My last stop was to see Aunt Lena. For sure she would be at *Cannoli's,* baking her heart out. I followed the intoxicating aromas of chocolate and vanilla and sure enough found her in the bakery's kitchen. She had flour on her hands and streaks of chocolate on her apron.

She pursed her lips upon seeing me. "Ed said you might stop in." She plated a pretty chocolate cupcake topped with white frosting and chocolate streaks. "Eat. Then talk."

Ordinarily, I'd go to *Cannoli's* hoping to grab a cupcake or a brownie. Today, I doubted I could eat anything. But she was watching me so I peeled the paper off the cupcake and took a bite. The cake's moistness helped it go down my throat easier than I'd have thought. But I couldn't manage a second bite.

Aunt Lena dusted off her hands and poured me a glass of water. "Ed told me you have a meeting with some big shot this evening."

I nodded and to my surprise, my eyes filled with tears. *Weakling! Coward!*

My aunt clucked like a mother hen and pulled me into her meaty arms. "Whatever or whoever you're going to face, you'll come out fine. Your mother and Frank didn't raise you to be brave, but they raised you to be smart. And strong-willed. You'll get the best of this." She let go of me and squeezed my chin with her hand. "You'll do whatever you need to. If I could, I'd go with you and help, but—"

Blinking back tears, I interrupted, "But you have a husband to take care of and cakes to bake." I attempted a giggle.

"I was gonna say, I'm too old to wrestle gangsters, but I like what you said better." She picked up the rest of my cupcake. "Now, finish this, and I'll get you a new chocolate butterscotch bar I'm trying out."

In the time it took for her to grab one of the bars and hand it to me, what she'd said sunk in. She was right. I could do whatever I set my mind to. I'd proven that over and again. One bite of the butterscotch bar reminded me that, no matter what else happened, I wanted to go on living just so I could have more of those luscious treats my aunt baked.

I spent the remainder of my free time with my aunt, listening to her good-humored banter with Angie, her best friend, about which cookies they should bake the following day. I just hoped I'd be above ground to taste them.

ဆဩ

I FELT STRANGELY CALM on my way to meeting Corrigan. Maybe the intensity of the chocolate I'd eaten was affecting me. Most likely, though, it was my aunt. I silently thanked God for her.

Inside the police station, I spotted Corrigan who was in deep conversation with a man I'd never seen before. Corrigan glanced up and motioned to me. "Claire, come on over here." He introduced me to the other guy, Bill, who I learned worked with electronics.

"Let's go into Interrogation Room Three." Corrigan led the way.

I attempted some lame humor. "Sure, you only let me see room three. Are the other rooms secret?" I didn't exactly expect any guffaws, but Bill merely looked quizzically and Corrigan just grunted.

"Have a seat, Claire." Corrigan sat across from me in the room, while Bill fiddled with some equipment. He picked up an almost invisible silver thing.

"That's what I'll be wearing?"

Bill nodded. "Yep. We'll be able to hear you loud and clear with this baby."

ℰℭ

I HAD THE MICROPHONE in place along with sincere assurances from Corrigan that he'd be able to hear everything Bucanetti and I said. He insisted nothing would go wrong, but in the off chance it did, he would be nearby. All I needed now was the fortitude to meet with Bucanetti.

On my jacket, Corrigan carefully pinned an ugly piece of costume jewelry that concealed the microphone "Okay, Claire. You're hooked up and ready to go. Remember, lead him to confessing. If you can't get him there, don't do anything foolish. We'll figure out another way."

I nodded, barely hearing him. I dug deeply within myself. It was either this, or spending my life eating prison food. This meeting or having to give up Charlie. I pushed my brain in this either/or direction all the way to Corsi's Italian Restaurant, a family-owned business that'd been around since before my parents dated.

Corrigan and Abby took off from the station before I did. They wanted to get positioned near enough to the restaurant to get to me fast if need be. Thirty minutes after they left, Bill signaled for me to take off. My feet felt as if someone had filled my shoes with cement. I made it to my car and started it up.

Rush hour traffic had ended a while ago, so I was able

to get to Murray Hill in forty minutes. Finding a parking spot was more challenging. I felt my forehead moisten and my hands sweat as I drove around looking for a place to put my car. Finally, a spot opened up, but I'm not great at parallel parking and so took even more time trying to fit somewhat close to the curb. By the time I'd accomplished that, I was a big sweaty mess.

I took a second to compose myself and go over in my mind what I planned on saying to Bucanetti. I wanted him to admit to hiring Eileen not only to kill Paul, but also Pilkosky. In the most positive way of thinking, I'd get him to do both without a drop of blood being shed. My blood.

Praying silently, I managed to get myself out of my car and into the restaurant, an old-style Italian place that still had the red-flocked paper and pictures of old Italian mamas everywhere. The place looked empty and I began to think Bucanetti had stood me up. Until the maître d' approached me. He looked about forty and seemed as uneasy as me.

"Mr. Bucanetti is waiting for you. Please follow me." He led me to a back corner of the restaurant and there sat the gangster big as life, his back to the wall, eating a plate of veal parmesan.

Bucanetti delicately wiped his mouth. He smirked at me. "Well, if it isn't little Miss DeNardo. Jimmy, pat her down."

Jimmy, the maître d', shifted from one foot to another, then quickly went through the motions of frisking me. Thank goodness he was old school and wasn't able to detect the equipment I wore. Still, I held my breath, hoping he wouldn't chance upon the miniscule microphone in my pin.

I breathed a bit easier when Jimmy declared me clean. Bucanetti motioned to the chair opposite him.

I looked around, but Jimmy had vanished so quickly I wondered if he'd been real. "Thank you." I sat on the edge of the designated chair, knowing the trial of my life was now beginning.

Chapter Nineteen

HOPE YOU DON'T mind me eating while you're talking, Miss DeNardo." He clearly wasn't going to stop forking the pasta that accompanied the veal parmesan into his mouth no matter what I said. "You know, food is love. And I love food." He chuckled at his witticism, but there was no humor in it and his dark eyes were as soul-dead as ever.

I bluffed, "I don't mind, but you may lose your appetite after our conversation."

"Doubtful, but let's talk. Tommy said you claim to have something I want."

I hoped Corrigan could hear me loud and clear. "I know who really killed Paul Morley and who was behind it all."

He carefully laid his fork and knife onto his empty plate. His upper lip curled. "You're the one who killed him. Isn't that what they say?"

A drop of perspiration slid down between my breasts and I wondered if it could short out the wires. "Yes, but rather than go to the cops with my information, I thought you and I should talk."

"And why is that?"

I took a deep breath to calm myself. "Are you acquainted with Mandy Williams, aka Eileen Murphy?"

His eyes opened just a fraction wider. "Can't say as I am."

I reminded myself to ask open-ended questions. "What sort of business did you and Paul Morley do together?"

He sat back in his chair. "Morley handled a few legal cases for me. That's it."

"Mind if I have some water?" My mouth was getting drier than a piece of beef jerky.

"Take mine. I haven't touched it." He slid the sweating glass over toward me.

"Thank you." I sipped it, hoping it contained nothing other than water and ice. My tongue worked again. "I didn't kill Paul and you know it. In fact, I know who killed him and who set the whole thing in motion. I just don't know why."

Bucanetti gripped the edge of the table. "So, again, why are you here? I thought we'd agreed you'd stay out of my way. In exchange, you and your family would stay safe. Now you're here hinting about some murder." He leaned toward me and I could smell the sauce and wine on his breath. "You got something to say, say it."

Despite my best intentions to stay calm, I blurted out,

"You hired Eileen Murphy to kill Paul Morley and pin it on me."

His face morphed into a mask of rage. "Who the hell do—"

Heavy footsteps pounded behind me. A deep voice interrupted Bucanetti. "Boss, look what we found sittin' nearby. Listening."

I spun around feeling as if I'd pass out. A tall, husky man whose shirt was busting at the seams had a gun pointed at Corrigan's head. Another slightly shorter man held Corrigan's arms behind his back.

Abby was nowhere around and my worst fear was that they'd killed her.

Bucanetti's face turned a mottled color and for a moment he said nothing. Then, glaring at me, he told one of his goons, "Tony, she's wired up. Get rid of it."

I tried to resist, but his goon ripped my jacket off. He found what he was looking for and smashed it.

"Claire DeNardo and Detective Corrigan." Bucanetti's voice dripped with venom. "You were dumb enough to think I'd confess to killing Morley and you'd have it all recorded." He pounded so hard on the table the silverware jumped.

Tony spoke up. "What do you want us to do with them?"

Again, Bucanetti was silent. Then he started his voice lower, gravelly and dangerous. "Tell ya what. You wanna know what happened? I ordered Eileen Murphy to kill that phony hustler. He thought he could skim money from me…”

He squinted, then his eyes darkened. “Tony, Rocco, put these two in the car out back. They'll have an unfortunate accident.” He grabbed the bottle of wine on his table. “Wait.” He splashed the liquid onto Corrigan. He chuckled, but there wasn't any humor behind it. “You know, you shouldn't drink and drive.”

Even if I was going to die, I had to know. “Wait! First, before you do anything, did you also kill Ben Pilkosky?”

“I'll tell you so you can die in peace. No. That fool crook got offed by somebody else. Tony, Rocco, get ‘em outta here.”

Rocco placed his hands under my arms and lifted me up. I struggled, holding onto the chair as if it were a part of me. I suddenly let go and sprang into action, grabbing the knife from the table and slashing wildly at his hands.

I hit my target and Rocco dropped me. I spun around and jabbed again. This time I was able to graze his chest, but I didn't do any serious damage. Rocco snatched the knife from my hand and slapped me for good measure. I placed my hand against my cheek, foolishly thinking how it would bruise. As if that was my worst problem. Rocco grabbed my arm, squeezing it so tightly, I winced.

Meanwhile Tony, who'd been watching Corrigan, chuckled at my pain and so got distracted. Corrigan saw his chance and the two struggled for Tony's gun.

“Enough!” Bucanetti was standing, his own weapon pointed at Corrigan and me. “Everyone take it easy. Tony, take your gun.”

Bucanetti sneered, "Now, this is gonna go down like I said."

From the corner of my eye, I saw a cook wearing a chef's toque or tall hat, nonchalantly approaching us with a soup tureen, as if this was the most expected thing at this moment.

Bucanetti turned ever so slightly. "What the hell?" The chef skidded to a halt and threw the tureen of scalding Italian wedding soup straight at the mobster's face. Bucanetti screamed and dropped his revolver. His hands flew to his face.

Seizing the opportunity, Corrigan wrestled the distracted Tony for his pistol while the chef dove onto Rocco. Rocco's knife flew from his hand, and I pounced on the gun Bucanetti had dropped. The next moments were a blur, but at last, I cocked the hand gun and yelled, "It's over." Police sirens were getting closer.

Corrigan used Tony's gun to cover Rocco and Tony while I kept an eye on Bucanetti, who screamed he needed a doctor. Holding his own weapon on him, I dabbed cool water from the glass onto his reddened face. "We'll get you a doctor. Most likely a prison doctor."

To my surprise, I felt sorry that he'd been burned. Funny, since he'd have no qualms about killing me.

Without turning I asked Ed, "How did you get in here?"

A commotion prevented him from answering. It was Abby pushing the handcuffed maître d' and uniformed officers were right behind her. All armed and ready to take

Bucanetti and his associates into custody.

With Bucanetti, cuffed, an EMT applied salve to his face, and he bandaged Rocco's hand. They were being escorted away but the mob boss stopped and gave me a cold-fish look. "I'm gonna beat this. We're not done."

I swallowed and pushed down my fears that he was right. I'd deal with that another day.

Abby holstered her gun and turned to Corrigan. "I got out of the car long enough to find a bathroom and get some coffee. When I returned, you were gone. I called for backup and headed inside. I got delayed by the maître d'." She looked at Ed and me. Grudgingly, she admitted, "Looks like you handled it fine without me. I never would've believed it."

Corrigan grinned like a pennant-winning baseball coach. "Claire, you were great! You too, Ed."

I thanked Corrigan and turned to Ed. "Again, how did you manage to get in here?"

With a crooked smile, he chuckled, "It pays to have a wife who knows everyone in the Cleveland food business. I told her what was gonna happen. She called a friend who works here in the kitchen. Next thing I know, I'm wearing a chef's outfit and being introduced as the new cook."

After we all made our statements to the police, Ed and I were free to go, although we would be called upon later. Ed patted my shoulder. "You did good, kiddo. I'm going home to my wife. Wanna come too?"

The danger and excitement over, my body felt as if it'd sprung a leak allowing all my energy to drain out.

"Thanks, Ed, but I'm going home and hugging Charlie. Please thank Aunt Lena for her intervention."

Ed glanced over at Corrigan, who was still talking to Abby. "Sure. Maybe you want to talk to Brian before you go."

I spun around at the same time Corrigan did and our eyes met. Not exactly a romantic moment, though, because as I turned, something flew into my left eye, a hair, piece of dust, something. I started blinking madly followed by my eye watering freely.

Corrigan walked over to me and handed me a handkerchief. He joked, "I didn't know looking at me could bring you to tears."

I dabbed at my eye, knowing any mascara and eyeliner I'd been wearing was now trailing down my cheeks. "Thanks." I looked down at the makeup stained cloth. "I'll wash this and get it back to you."

"No problem. Keep it as a souvenir."

"Of one of the times I almost got killed?"

He put his hands over mine. "Of the time I finally realized how good you are at what you do."

My exhaustion disappeared. Out of the side of my mouth, I whispered, "You're not so bad yourself."

We both stood there, smiling at each other. Until Abby called him over with questions. Since the police were done with me for the time being, I slipped away, content with Corrigan's comments and getting the bad guy. Let's face it, though. The best thing was that charges against me would be dropped. I'd be a free woman at last.

That contentment didn't last long. In fact, it only lasted until I had my seatbelt on.

Bucanetti admitted to hiring Eileen Murphy to kill Paul. But what about Ben Pilkosky? Who killed him? A part of me wanted to just forget it. For just a day, to celebrate my freedom. But part of me just couldn't. Nadia was still the main suspect for Pilkosky's murder. I'd promised her I'd help and I couldn't ignore that promise.

Chapter Twenty

I STRUGGLED BETWEEN going home and going to my office. It was already ten and the energy I had left made me envious of a sloth. I made a right hand turn onto the freeway. Home it would be.

By the time I parked my car and dragged myself to my apartment, all I could think of was bed. Charlie would need a walk, of course, but then, bed.

Surprisingly, the cool evening air perked me up along with my appetite. I thought longingly of the chicken cacciatore in my office fridge. If it hadn't been so late, I'd have driven over there. Instead, I made do with a handful of stale cashews and tumbled into bed.

I couldn't have been there more than ten minutes when my phone rang. Harold.

"Claire! I just heard the good news. Congratulations. I was completing my defense strategy for you when I found out Mr. Bucanetti got arrested. The prosecutor will surely dismiss your case."

I stifled a yawn. "I hope so. Thank you for calling, Harold." My eyelids drooped.

"Of course, I'll start the process of having your arrest expunged from your record. That will take a few months. Why don't we keep our appointment for next Friday?"

Dollar signs instead of sheep jumped over a green hedge. I wondered what my final bill would be. "Sure. Fine. Good night, Harold."

"Claire, wait! Now that you have more free time, perhaps you can devote some of it to helping my other client. As you promised."

I groaned like a teenager given a curfew. "Okay, you're right. I'll start first thing in the morning. If I solve the murder and get Nadia off, shouldn't you give me a discount, say twenty percent off my bill?"

He scoffed. "Oh, Claire! I cannot believe you're negotiating with me."

"Well, what about it?"

"We'll see." Before I could argue, he ended the call.

I went back to bed. My head hit the pillow again and that was it.

सॐ

FUNNY HOW MY conscience works. It was still dark outside when it woke me up. I was sleeping in my own bed, while Nadia was…Where? Probably back in jail, her bail most likely revoked for commission of another crime.

I mentally beat myself up for not paying more attention to her.

I rose from my bed, threw some water on my face and brushed my teeth. I guessed my brain had registered 'first thing in the morning' as three in the morning. I sighed and slipped out to the kitchen. I made myself a cup of tea and waited for my computer to boot up.

My tea cooled while I read everything I could about the Pilkosky murder. As it stood, Nadia didn't have a chance to be found innocent. I'd have to drag Ed into this investigation. I hated to do it, since he'd worked so hard and I wasn't sure I would be able to pay him. Since I'd been charged with Paul's murder, my business had gone down the drain. Panicking, I checked my bank balance. With its paltry amount, I doubted I'd be able to even afford ramen noodles.

Charlie was now up and ready to go outside. I closed down my computer, threw a jacket on and complied with his wishes. That accomplished, I'd feed him and then get ready for the day.

Why plans are called plans, I don't know. Because nothing ever goes as planned. The minute I walked out of my building, my phone rang. It was Corrigan. The man must never sleep.

"Claire, I know it's early, but they just brought Dylan Morley in. He probably didn't have anything to do with his father's murder, but we're booking him for locking you in that closet. That's false imprisonment. We need you to come down to make your statement."

Charlie was sniffing around to find his special spot. "Thanks. I do need to talk to Dylan about his father's dealings with Ben Pilkosky. If Charlie hurries up, I can be there in an hour."

"That'll work. Dylan will be here a long time."

A few pleasantries later, Charlie located his spot. Then he looked up at me, as if to say, "I did good. Now feed me."

I patted his head. "Will do, Mr. Charlie."

⅏

MY DOGGY CHORES and a scant amount of personal grooming finally done, I made it to the police station in a bit over an hour. Despite it being only six in the morning, the place was bustling with activity.

Corrigan spotted me, though, and hustled over. I'm sure I looked as if I'd been at a rave for twenty-four hours. Unbelievably, he looked as fresh as those men's soap commercials.

"It's good to see you again, Claire." His smile faded quickly and he turned to the business at hand. "Have a seat." He motioned to the chair by Abby's desk.

"Okay, but after I give my statement and answer all your questions, remember, I want to talk to Dylan myself. I need to find out more about his father and Ben Pilkosky."

Corrigan rubbed his chin. "I didn't forget, but we've got Pilkosky's killer. I know you believe otherwise, but the evidence points to your former cellmate." I raised my chin, ready to argue. "Okay, Claire. I'll give you a chance to talk with him. But I'll need to be present."

"Fine by me." I smirked. "Maybe you can pick up some pointers on how to interrogate a suspect."

He chuckled, "Looks as if you're getting cocky since you handled Bucanetti so well yesterday."

My eyebrows rose, but I didn't respond because Abby sat down across from me. I gave her my statement. Satisfied, she turned me back over to Corrigan. "She's all yours, Brian." Her voice dropped and she added bitterly, "But then, that's what he's wanted all along."

I did a double take, but I don't think Corrigan heard the end part.

Corrigan said, "Okay, Dylan is sitting in room three with his lawyer. He's agreed to answer your questions as long as it doesn't implicate him in any crime."

Dylan looked thinner than I remembered and a lot shaggier. "Hello, Dylan."

"Hi, Claire. Say, I'm sorry about what I did. I mean, I didn't want anything bad to happen to you…" His lawyer shook his head a fraction and Dylan stopped.

I waved his apology aside. "I'm sorry you're where you are, but I'm not here to talk about putting me in the closet. I want to talk to you about Benjamin Pilkosky."

He sat up straight. "What about him?"

I chewed on my lower lip for a second, thinking. "You knew your family's money wasn't safe with him."

Dylan flinched. "Yeah, I suspected as much. But I didn't kill the guy! I swear!"

Corrigan interrupted. "What do you know about the victim's death?"

Dylan's lawyer nodded, but the prisoner looked ready to cry. "Whatever was on the news. I lived under the radar, not in a cave. And that day I was with some of the other men at the center. At least one of them could vouch for me."

Corrigan shoved a pad of paper toward Dylan and a pen. "We'll need their names and some way of contacting them."

This was my interrogation, so I gave Corrigan a look that told him to step back. "Look, Dylan, I don't think you did it. Okay? I just want to know if you have any idea who would do such a thing."

He picked up the pen and played with it. "Have you talked to my sister, Janette?"

My hearing sharpened. "Why do you say that?"

He leaned in. "She'd do anything for that money. I bet she'd even kill somebody to get her hands on it."

Corrigan again spoke. "What about anyone else?"

Dylan shook his head. "Nope." He paused then he turned toward me, his voice almost breaking. "Will you tell Sarah for me that I'm really sorry I screwed up. Tell her I love her. Please."

"I'll do what I can, Dylan." I ignored Corrigan's stern look.

Dylan's attorney spoke up. "This interview is over, folks."

Corrigan stood. "Not until I get that list of people who

could vouch for your whereabouts."

Dylan quickly scribbled a few names and handed it to Corrigan. "I don't know addresses. They're mostly homeless."

Though Dylan had a lot to answer for, before I exited, I wished him good luck. He seemed surprised, but thanked me.

Outside the interrogation room, I asked Corrigan where Sarah was now. "You didn't want to press charges against her. Case was dropped. I assume she's back home."

"I'll give her Dylan's message later. Did you ever interview Janette Morley for Pilkosky's murder?"

Corrigan huffed. "No. No need for it." His eyebrows lowered. "Wait a minute. If you're thinking of questioning Janette Morley, forget it. That's something the police will do."

"Oh! All of a sudden it's a police matter. It just occurred to you now to follow up on this particular suspect. Something you should have done earlier." I wasn't in the mood to be charming or diplomatic.

This time that tiny vein in his temple belly-danced. "The primary suspect has been charged. We have motive and opportunity. We don't have the murder weapon, but that's bound to turn up."

Here we go. The same old arguments. "You'll forgive me if I mention that this wouldn't be the first time you've arrested the wrong person."

I fully expected him to shoot back some belittling

comment. He didn't. Instead, he grabbed my hand and stumbled over his next words. "You're right. I haven't always…been right. If you're convinced she's Pilkosky's killer, then I'll follow up on your suspicions."

I jerked my head back. *He just admitted he's been wrong!* "I think we—"

One of the officers tapped Corrigan on the shoulder. "Detective Corrigan, you got a call. Eileen Murphy woke up."

I never finished my sentence because it seemed as if everyone sprang into action with that news. Glancing around, I could tell nobody, including Corrigan, was interested in what I had to say. I slipped out of the station virtually unnoticed.

Determined to talk with Janette before the cops did, the minute I got into my car, I called the number she'd given me. It wasn't a matter of me wanting to be a hero. It was that I wanted, needed, Corrigan to see I was as good at my job as he was at his. Besides, I'd promised Nadia I'd help her and this was the best way I could do it.

To my great relief, she answered on the first ring. "This is Janette Morley. And, Claire, you better have some good news for me."

I fought the urge to start blabbing about how I practically solved her father's murder. "I have a lot of good news for you. How about I share it this afternoon?"

"Of course. Why don't we meet at the usual place?"

"Usual place?"

With a bit of impatience, she responded, "You know.

The Tango Room."

I glanced at the time. Noon. "Oh, sure. The name of the place just slipped my mind for a minute."

"Meet me there at twelve thirty." She ended the call before I could ask for a bit more time. I'd been in such a hurry to talk to Dylan, I'd thrown on a previously worn pair of jeans and an orange top that made me look like a tangerine. It would take me almost half an hour to get to the Tango Room. I had no choice but to freshen up in the bar's restroom before I met with Janette.

It was already twenty after twelve when I parked and walked through Tango Room's door. I made a beeline to the ladies' room, hoping Janette hadn't seen me. One look in the mirror told me it'd take more than ten minutes to fix myself up, but I did the best I could, applying lipstick that unfortunately clashed with the color I was wearing.

I was running my fingers through my hair when Janette entered the restroom. She glanced at me and patted one of her stray hairs into place saying, "Oh, my dear. Face it. Nothing is going to help the way you look."

I bit my lip to stop me from cranking out a nasty retort. I needed her cooperation. My mouth controlled, I suggested we have a seat at her preferred table.

From behind the bar, our server hurried over to us. "Good afternoon, Ms. Morley. Your usual?"

"Yes, and bring *her*," she looked down her nose at me. "A chocolate martini. Nobody drinks those anymore but you can see she's not exactly a fashion maven."

I wanted to jump over the table and strangle this

obnoxious woman, but again I let her comment slide. I'd zing her with my questions.

Once we were alone again, I began. "First, if you haven't already heard, we've identified who the police and I believe really killed your father."

"Is that a fact? And it was my brother, correct?"

"No. It was someone hired by Michael Bucanetti, who you know is an alleged big time mobster. Your father, it seems, was involved with some of the guy's dealings."

She actually looked bored. "Well, Daddy wasn't always as clever as he believed he was." She stared at her manicured, polished nails. "Too bad Dylan wasn't the killer. That way he'd be out of my way."

"The police did find your brother. He's being charged with false imprisonment. He could face a year of prison."

The server brought our drinks and Janette took a long swallow of hers. "Oh, goody. A jailbird for a brother!" She shrugged. "Oh well, on the plus side, I won't have to split any inheritance with him for at least as long as he's in jail. Please tell me that simpering waif he calls his lover is also arrested."

I sipped my drink. It was delicious, rich and strong. I'd have to pace myself. "No, she's not." I didn't tell her about the charges being dropped against Dylan's girlfriend. "So, you know Sarah?"

Janette waved her hand as if swatting a fly. "A do-gooder who would do almost anything for my brother. Wants to marry him, God knows why. I swear, she's like a rescue puppy." Another long sip. "Anything else?" She picked up her purse.

I silently cursed myself for letting the conversation get away from me. "By the way, from what I hear, there isn't much inheritance left, since Ben Pilkosky dipped into it."

"That slime!"A drop of spittle formed in the corner of her mouth. "I wish he'd been flayed and quartered before he was killed. No doubt, though, the killer didn't have the time." She opened, then snapped her purse closed hard enough for the latch to bounce. She finished her drink and wiped her mouth.

"Is that all or, is there more?"

I blinked hard. The drink was already making me a bit lightheaded. "Where were you between seven and nine in the morning Pilkosky was killed?"

She sneered. "I don't have to account to you." She pulled out her wallet and called the server over. "Here. Put these drinks on my card. Quickly please."

The waitress took the card and hurried away. Janette hissed, "I didn't kill that jowly snake. That's all you need to know." Tight-lipped, she tapped her foot until the waitress returned with her credit card.

Janette pushed her chair back while stowing away her returned credit card. "I don't owe you anything. Leave me alone or I'll have you arrested for harassment." Her heels clicked loudly as she left the Tango Room.

I sat back, my face in my hands. So much for being good or better than Corrigan at interviewing. I pushed my drink away and hurried from the bar to my car. There had to be another way to go about this. Unfortunately, my brain was fried and the only thing it screamed was defeat. But that wasn't an option. Not now, not after my promise. And, I had to admit, for my own pride. Somehow I had to get the truth from Janette. Soon.

Chapter Twenty-One

THE EVENTS OF the past days, coupled with nights of little sleep, caught up with me. By the time I reached my apartment, I decided a nap wasn't out of the question. Afterwards, I'd have a clear mind, able to get to the truth of Janette's whereabouts when Pilkosky died.

I must have slept longer than I'd planned because it was dark outside when somebody banged on my door.

"Claire, open up. It's me, Brian."

I barely heard him what with Charlie barking and running in circles. I glanced down at myself, wrinkled clothes and a crease on my face where I'd slept on it. It'd have to do. I opened the door. Holding Charlie so he wouldn't bust out, I demanded, "What are you doing here?"

Before answering, he bent down and reached in far enough to pet Charlie. "Hi, boy. How you doin'?" Straightening, he addressed me. "I wanted to be the first to tell you. Eileen Murphy made a deathbed confession that Bucanetti hired her to kill Morley. The D.A. is dismissing the case against you."

I covered my face with my hands and jumped up and down, giddy. And relieved. "Oh! That's wonderful!" I felt as if I were light enough to float. "Thank you, Brian!" Without thinking, I hugged him.

He stiffened. "Uh, you're welcome."

I dropped my arms as if they had anvils attached. "Sorry. I just got excited."

"No. Nothing to be sorry about." He rubbed his face. "It's just the last time we hugged, we broke up."

I shut my eyes and wished I could disappear. I scolded myself for ruining a happy moment. "Yeah, I remember." Trying to bring back the elation, I looked up at him and smiled. "But this is a good moment, and we did it. Together."

He smiled back but his voice was wistful. "You're right. Together." He crouched down to pet Charlie again, who welcomed his attention.

I dug my nails into my hands. Better to feel some pain than to throw my arms around him again, which is what every fiber of me wanted to do. The fierceness of that feeling surprised me, and not knowing what to do about it, I stooped down to join Corrigan in petting Charlie. Good ole Charlie.

Corrigan rose first. "I better go. I haven't forgotten my promise to go talk to Janette Morley about where she was when Pilkosky was killed."

My face must have gotten as red as a stop sign. Corrigan groaned. "Don't tell me. You already talked to her. How? When?" I opened my mouth to answer, but he put his index finger to my mouth. "Never mind. What did you get from her?"

I couldn't believe he wasn't going to reprimand me or go into a tirade. "She refused to answer. Said I had no authority to make her tell me. Which leads me to think she has something to hide."

His voice turned thoughtful. "Or, she didn't think it was any of your business. I'll get an answer from her."

"I suppose you won't let me go with you. I could even wait in the car."

 He chortled. "No, but I'll call you as soon as I get her answer."

Impatient, I tugged on his sleeve and turning toward the door, urged, "Then go. As we speak she's probably putting together some phony alibi."

He backed out. "Okay, I'm going."

Alone again, I sighed. Things had changed so much. First, Corrigan was finally acting as if he trusted me to help solve a case. As if I was competent. I smiled to myself. Then I smiled at Charlie. "We both like him a lot, don't we Charlie?"

Feeling grungy, I showered and while brushing my teeth, I realized I was at loose ends. I hated waiting to see what information Corrigan pulled from Janette. It was too much like those women who waited for their husbands to come back from sea. I needed to do *something*.

Going back to my office seemed like the place to start. Maybe I'd uncover a clue I'd missed in my hurry to solve Pilkosky's murder.

Being Sunday, the building, including my office, was tomb-like quiet. I turned on my computer and began reviewing all my notes. My office phone ringing startled me. *Corrigan? So soon?*

It wasn't Corrigan, though. "Is this C. DeNardo?" I didn't recognize the man's voice.

"Yes, it is. May I ask who's calling?"

"My name is Mario Wilson and I'd like to make an appointment with this C. DeNardo."

A new client! Not wanting to scare him off, I toned down my excitement. "And what is this in regards to?"

"I think my wife is stepping out on me."

"Sorry to hear that." I took down his information and we settled on meeting Monday morning. The call ended and, for the first time in a while I felt optimistic about my business. I could get back to work. Maybe get more clients again.

Unfortunately, it didn't take long until that rosy cloud turned dark. I went through my neglected mail. Overdue bills, final notices, all sank me lower and lower.

As if that weren't enough, Corrigan hadn't called about Janette. I dragged myself out from under the pile of bills I couldn't possibly pay, and headed out the door.

On the way home I stopped at *Cannoli's* to have something chocolate. And maybe a sympathetic ear.

Aunt Lena was in *Cannoli's* kitchen, frosting a cake

somebody ordered for a baptism. She lifted her head up long enough to greet me with her usual pleasantness. "Claire, what are you doing here?"

I leaned against one of the counters. I didn't want to mope in front of her, so I hid my despondency behind a smile. "Oh, I just thought I'd drop by. See if you have any cookies or anything you'd like me to try."

She snorted. "You got a broken bone or something?"

"What? No. Why?"

"You never stop by just to taste test. Or to gab." She stopped, holding the icing cone mid-air. "What's wrong, sweetie?"

My false cheer collapsed like meringue in a hot room. "I'm feeling so overwhelmed right now. Business is so bad I'm afraid they'll turn out the lights and turn off the heat. How will I pay you and Dad back if my agency goes bankrupt?" My voice broke.

Aunt Lena didn't say anything. Instead, she laid down the icing cone and stepped over to a layer cake iced in milk chocolate and drizzled in dark chocolate. She silently cut a monstrous piece and slid it on a plate. "Here. Eat."

Whoever coined the phrase, 'food is love' must have known Aunt Lena. One bite of this exquisitely dense marbled cake and my worries drifted away. Not far away, but enough of a distance to allow me to smile for real. "Mmm! Thanks, Aunt Lena."

"She gave me a one-armed hug. "You're no quitter and I just know you'll be fine. You got a family who loves you and a good man who does too." She released me. "Now finish that slice. You want some water?"

I tried to say yes, but my mouth was full so I just nodded. I felt better with each bite. Chocolate makes me feel good. Being loved makes me feel fantastic.

Fully sated, I thanked Aunt Lena and headed home. In the ten minutes it took me to get there, I nearly convinced myself she was right and I'd be okay. Opening my apartment door, I was greeted by Charlie, licking my face. He probably smelled the cake on me. My dog helped me stay hopeful. He always does.

℘)CR

CHARLIE AND I SETTLED down on the sofa, watching some mindless movie about a romance gone wrong. I still hadn't heard from Corrigan by the time it was over. I picked my phone and laid it down several times, not wanting to call him if he had no news, but I couldn't help myself. "Brian?" I could hear chaos in the background.

"Claire, I can't talk. I'm on my way to W. 40th. Multiple shooters. Stay away from the area."

"Be care—"

He cut me off, adding, "Her alibi's the partner."

"What?" But he'd ended the call. My hand flew to my mouth. Two questions fought to be uppermost. Partner? And, would Corrigan be okay?

I pushed any concern about Corrigan away to solve the first question about the partner. Whose partner? I didn't think Janette had a partner. At least I didn't run across one when I dug into her life. But, her father did. He had a law partner. I drummed my fingers on my thigh, trying to remember his name. It finally came to me. Adam Bennett. Paul had mentioned him once. Apparently, he was a real man-about-town. Trying to recall that name distracted me for only a few minutes.

Then that second question about Corrigan's safety clawed its way to the front of my mind. A lump formed in my throat. He was going into a dangerous, unknowable situation. My hands shook as I flipped on the local news station. An announcer had broken into the program to say that there was a standoff between police and three gunmen who had held up a bank downtown. They were holding four hostages.

Charlie hopped onto the sofa and I latched on to him, my eyes glued to the television screen. I watched as the cops and those in authority moved stealthily, hunched over behind barriers. One policeman had been killed. Two more injured. No names released yet. I chewed on my cuticles, something I haven't done since grade school.

When the reporter had nothing new to report I switched stations. I checked for information on my phone. There was nothing further. My stomach was knotted up. Prayers poured from my mouth. When I ran through the ones I knew, I started over.

I fidgeted with my phone and paced back and forth, waiting for updates. None came. To stop myself from imagining the worst, and since I was accomplishing nothing, I decided to investigate Adam Bennett, starting with his home address. Being a Sunday, maybe he was there.

My phone rang while I drove to Cleveland's Gold Coast and Adam Bennett's last known address. It was my dad. "Claire, I saw the news. Is Brian caught in that mess? Have you heard from him?"

I frowned and tried to keep any anxiousness from my voice. "Yes, he is, and no, not for a while. I'm sure he'll be okay, Dad. He knows how to take care of himself." If only I believed the words I was spouting.

His voice was a battle between calm and worry. "Yeah, you're right. He knows what he's doing. Call me if you hear anything. Promise?"

"Sure, Dad." Another call was beeping in as this one ended. "Hello?"

"Claire, it's your aunt. Ed told me. Is Brian okay?"

I closed my eyes and exhaled. "I hope so. I talked to him just before he arrived on the scene."

"Well, me and Angie are praying. I'll say a rosary and light a candle as soon as I can. But you let me know the second you hear something."

"I will, Aunt Lena."

She huffed. "Maybe this is a good thing."

Horrified, I yelled, "What?"

"I mean, maybe you'll realize what it could be like without Brian. You know, you can't wait forever to decide you want him."

My shoulders rose and I gripped my steering wheel as if it were her arm. "This isn't the time to talk about that.

I've got to go-love-you-bye."

My thoughts were so black I couldn't form a sane idea for a few seconds. How could this be a good thing? My aunt must be inhaling too much vanilla.

Reaching my destination, I loosened my grip on the steering wheel and relaxed. Corrigan had been in other dangerous situations before. Why had it not bothered me then? Was I so caught up in proving myself professionally I didn't think about it? I wrinkled my nose as if I'd smelled something foul. I hadn't been worried before because he was my competition. Not that he'd take business from me, but I always felt like the underdog. So much to prove. Now, though, it seemed that we were friends and allies. And it felt good. So good. But, if that was gone, if he were killed? My arms made an X across my chest and I leaned forward, as if to protect my heart from being badly bruised. The realization that I loved Corrigan rose from my gut. *Please, God, let him be okay.*

Somebody knocked on my driver's side window, startling me. It was the parking lot attendant. "Are you okay, lady?"

I lowered my window. "Yes. Yes, I'm fine. Ah, is this the parking lot for the Lake Condos?"

"Yeah, but visitors need to park back there." He pointed with a flashlight.

I thanked him and moved my car. I put away as best I could my worries about Corrigan. I still had a job to do.

Chapter Twenty-Two

I SLIPPED INTO THE condominium as a woman went out. I moved down the hall until I arrived at Adam Bennett's place. I rang his doorbell and a butler answered. "Is Mr. Bennett expecting you?"

In my most official voice, I responded, "It's regarding Janette Morley. I'm sure he'll see me."

From around the corner into the foyer, a middle-aged man with full brown-turning-gray hair and a day's worth of beard appeared. "Can I help you?" His voice was rich and attention-getting.

"Are you Adam Bennett?"

He turned to the butler. "I'll take it from here, Tennyson." He waited until we were alone to answer me. "Yes, I am." He looked me up and down, clearly disapproving. "Janette told me. I've been expecting a male detective."

"He's busy right now. I'm filling in for him. I'm a

private investigator."

He held up his hand. "It doesn't matter. I was with Janette Morley on that morning of the day in question. We were," he cleared his throat, "enjoying each other's company. I'll even swear to it if need be."

I bit my lower lip. "Where was this?"

He smirked. "Here. Tennyson can vouch for us." His smirk became a sneer. "I can show you the exact spot in the bedroom if you insist."

I banished the visual he was offering. "That's not necessary. Have you been in a relationship long?"

"Yes, and Paul knew about it, if that's what you're wondering. I think he even approved. Better than his son's choice. That little blonde who plays so innocent." He rubbed his chin. "Now, I have a glass of wine that's waiting for me. You can see yourself out."

My interest piqued, I asked, "What do you mean plays so innocent?"

His face was unreadable. "Just a feeling. Innocence is such an overrated quality. I wonder why anybody would hold onto it. Now, it's truly goodbye."

Frustrated, I replied, "Thank you for your cooperation," I exited and hurried to my car to check if there was any news about the standoff on W. 40th Street.

It was over. Two police dead, four wounded. The shooters, all three of them had been killed. Hostages were being treated and released. My hands shook trying to punch in Corrigan's number. I didn't have to, though. He called me. It took me three swipes to answer. "Are you all right?"

"Yeah. I was lucky. A bullet grazed my arm, but it's just a scratch."

I could feel the tension in my body melt away, and I quickly sent up a silent prayer of thanks. Through tears of relief I managed, "I'm so glad!"

He joked, "Thanks. I hope you're crying because you're happy."

"I'm thrilled." A need to touch him, to make sure he was truly okay surged through me. "When can I see you?"

"A few hours. I've gotta make a report. Then I'm gonna go home and change out of these clothes. I'll call you?"

"You don't need to change clothes. Just come over. Please." I almost added that he wouldn't stay long in those clothes anyway. But I didn't. I needed to slow myself down. Do nothing I could regret later.

He sounded exhausted. "That's the best thing I've heard all day. I'll be there in less than an hour."

Hurrying to make it home in time to meet Corrigan, I called my aunt and my dad to tell them the good news. Both were relieved and grateful I'd called. My aunt, of course, couldn't go without a bit of advice. "He called you right away. That shows how much he cares. Grab him while he's hot."

I groaned. "Aunt Lena, the expression is, 'while the iron is hot'".

"It doesn't matter. Latch on to him and don't let go. Or, a smarter and probably younger woman will do it.

Mark my words."

"Got it. Now, I have to go."

I'd reached my parking lot, turned off the car and practically ran into my apartment.

I greeted Charlie, then dashed around picking up my dirty clothes, stashing unwashed dishes and putting Charlie's toys in his basket. Finally done, I collapsed on the sofa, Charlie joining me. He had that look on his face that he needed to go out so I grabbed his leash and made it out of the apartment building door just in time for him to do what he needed.

Once back inside my apartment, I tried removing Charlie's leash. He began squirming so much, it was difficult. That meant only one thing. Corrigan had arrived.

My excitement rose too and I couldn't suppress a big, stupid smile from spreading across my face.

Corrigan knocked once and I swung the door open and, despite my resolution to play it cool, I practically jumped into his strong and welcoming arms.

Chapter Twenty-Three

I WOKE UP THE next morning snuggling with Charlie. Corrigan and I had approximately forty-five minutes together before he got called back into the station for more follow up. But that was enough to allow us to say everything that needed to be said.

I smiled widely and hugged Charlie. "I may very well be in love again." I announced to nobody. Charlie jumped off the bed and ran in a circle, excited. Even though it was probably because he wanted to go outside, I thanked him for being happy for me.

We made our usual rounds outside until he was finished, then we returned to my apartment for my own ministrations.

I was brushing my teeth when Corrigan called. "Hey, beautiful. What are you doing this morning?"

I rinsed my mouth. "I need to go into my office. I have an appointment with a potential new client. Why?"

"Thought I'd take you to breakfast. I get it, though. Business before pleasure."

I sighed. "Could we make it a lunch date instead?"

"Sure. The Courtyard Bistro at one?"

"I'm looking forward to it. Really."

"Me too. See you then."

The call ended and I felt somehow let down. Was it that without the danger I wasn't so much in love? I shook that idea out of my head, but a kernel of doubt lingered.

By the time I arrived at my office, I'd pushed back any thoughts about my relationship with Corrigan. I had to be clear minded for this morning's appointment. I transformed myself into the confident, clever detective this client would no doubt expect. I made all the papers I'd need available if the client signed on and crossed my fingers.

At precisely nine in the morning, a man in his fifties wearing a green work shirt and khakis came into my office. "I'm here to see Mr. DeNardo."

I extended my hand. "I'm C. DeNardo. Call me Claire." I motioned to the chair facing my desk.

He sat and rubbed his balding head. "I wasn't expecting a woman, but I guess it's okay by me."

"Good. Now, can you tell me more about what brought you in to see me?"

He patted his breast pocket, the sign of a man in need of a smoke. Most likely recalling he couldn't light up, he cracked his knuckles and began. "Maryann, that's my wife, always had dinner ready for me when I got home from work. We'd watch TV together. Not no more. Now she gets all fancied up, like a call girl or something and goes out gallivanting with this woman she met when she started volunteering. God knows where she gets the money to buy those things." He paused, rubbing his hand over his heavy beard. "What I wanna know is, where she goes and what she does with this new friend."

It sounded like a standard sob story; wife finds a fun new life sans husband. "I understand. I'd need a picture of your wife and this friend if you have one. Also, tell me whatever you know about this woman Maryann met."

He slumped back in his chair. "Alls I know is that my wife met her at the Westside Christian Center and her name is Sarah something-or-other." He pulled up a picture on his phone. "This is the best I could get of Maryann and her friend. This is her friend." He pointed at a blonde in the picture, her face obscured by her hair.

My hands clenched and my mouth went as dry as a desert breeze, but I managed to croak, "You're sure her name is Sarah?"

He went on, oblivious it seemed to my increased tension. "Yeah. Look, Maryann's a lot younger than me. And this Sarah's been filling her head with all kinds of bullsh—. Sorry. Nonsense about doing better than me." He laughed, a bitter, rage-filled sound. Then he leaned forward and placed his muscular forearms on my desk. "I just want my wife back and this Sarah out of her life. Can you do that? Can you see where they're going tonight?"

Allen Bennett's comment about Sarah's innocent act

flashed through my head. Now, Mario Wilson was drawing me the same picture. But was it really Dylan's Sarah? *Come on! How many other blonde Sarahs worked at the Center?* There seemed to be a lot more to Sarah Mueller than I'd originally thought. I chided myself for missing important clues. I'd fix that now by taking Wilson's case and investigating Sarah and of course, Maryann more thoroughly

"I can certainly find out more about your wife's activities for you." I quoted him my fees and after some minor quibbling, he agreed to them, signing all the required paperwork. Before he left, he provided me with his address, Maryann's cell phone number, and the photo of Maryann he'd shown me. The final action he took was my favorite. He wrote me a retainer check. Now, I could be assured of keeping my lights on.

I quickly escorted Mario to the door, desperately wanting to confront Sarah Mueller. I sighed heavily. It took all my willpower to not do that because I had to meet Corrigan for lunch. Besides, I told myself, Corrigan should be in on this.

I freshened up a bit and finally left for that lunch. I thought I'd be early, but as usual, Corrigan beat me there. He had even cleaned up. A crisp blue shirt that brought out his eyes and a suit that actually looked pressed. The best part was his broad smile upon seeing me.

We started with casual conversation that quickly turned to work topics. By the time we'd ordered, we were discussing my newest assignment. I ended with the name of the woman accompanying my client's wife.

Corrigan was leaning across the table, his eyes wide. "No kidding? Sarah Mueller? Who would've thought?"

Our meals arrived and we suspended shop talk to enjoy our food. He had a mound of fries and a Reuben sandwich, corned beef flopping out the sides of the bread and dripping with melted cheese. I had a salad, dressing on the side. I didn't resent his ability to eat all those calories. My reward awaited. We shared a piece of chocolate cheesecake with a thick chocolate ganache covering it. All that was surrounded by whipped cream. Taking a first, then second and third bite, I swore to myself I'd skip dinner.

The dishes cleared away, I brought up Sarah again. "I'm going to follow Maryann tonight and see where the duo goes. If I get some good photos, I'm sure Sarah will cooperate and tell me what she knows." Under my breath, I added, "Such as her whereabouts when Pilkosky was killed."

Corrigan held up his hands. "Whoa! Are you actually thinking she could have stabbed that guy?"

I twisted up my mouth. "She's small, but I think she's capable of doing anything she wants. Just like me." I placed my hands on my hips like a superhero.

He chuckled. "Okay, but leave the alibi questioning to the police. We'll be better equipped to check whatever she tells us."

After such a wonderful dessert, I didn't want to argue. "Just don't do anything until after tonight. I want to catch them red-handed. I'll have to have something to tell my client."

"It just so happens I'm up to my neck in other cases, so I won't get to it until tomorrow anyway."

Corrigan paid the bill and escorted me to my car. "Lunch was good. Thanks for meeting me. And for telling me about Sarah." With one hand against my car, he leaned in for a kiss. He tasted of chocolate. Even if it hadn't, his kiss was yummy. "Call me after your nighttime roaming. Good luck and be careful!"

I smiled. "I always am. Talk to you later." I slid into my car seat and he watched me drive away. I had to get ready for tailing Maryann and Sarah so I called Ed for company. I knew it'd be a long night.

Chapter Twenty-Four

ED AND I STARTED the evening sitting outside Maryann and Mario's home. It was twilight by the time Maryann walked out her door and got into a white Honda Accord. We followed the car down to the Flats, where they drove into the lot of Mick's Cleveland, a massive new gambling casino. We watched as driver and passenger valet parked and exited their vehicle. True to my expectations, Sarah Mueller was with Maryann Wilson. They were dressed in form-fitting, short dresses and the heels high enough to give me a nosebleed. I snapped a few pictures of them entering the casino. Ed stared at them and shook his head. "With those get-ups, they're looking for trouble."

I agreed. We self-parked and waited another five minutes. I brushed my hair in front of my face and yanked the brim of my hat down. Ed pulled up his collar and tipped down his cap. We walked into the casino and split up. He would cover Sarah, since she didn't know him.

The cacophonous bells and flashing lights of the slot machines disoriented me for a brief moment. Neither Maryann nor Sarah was in the main arena. Several smaller, fancier rooms branched out from the main gambling area. The first contained two crowded craps tables. The next, several blackjack tables. I spotted Maryann who had sidled up to a middle-aged man with chips stacked high in front of him. Though she had her hand on his arm, he ignored her and asked for another card, but once he revealed he'd been dealt more than twenty-one, a bust, he lightly patted her behind. "I thought you were gonna bring me luck, baby!" She pouted prettily and snuggled against the guy. I couldn't hear what she said, but he looked pleased.

I snapped picture after picture, until a tall man with a crew cut stopped me. "No taking pictures in this room." I tried pouting prettily but it didn't have the same effect as when Maryann did it to her target. This guy, dressed in a black suit, scowled and folded his arms across his chest, making sure I noticed the bulging muscles barely contained by his sleeves.

Reluctantly, I made my way out of the blackjack room, and I spotted Sarah talking to another man dressed like the one who'd warned me about taking pictures. Hearing their conversation in the noisy room from so far away was impossible. I ducked behind a row of slot machines, attempting to get closer. It was no use, but since I was out of their sight, I snapped a few pictures. She eventually moved to the last of the rooms off the main one. This was also the most elegant.

Four men and two women were playing baccarat, a fancy card game with a player and a banker. One man seemed to be doing very well. Without hesitation, Sarah slinked up to him and gave him a cunning, 'come-hither' smile.

Ed stood to the side, watching the game and Sarah intently. Not wanting to risk Sarah seeing me, I removed myself from the entrance of the room and returned to the slots. To kill time, I played a few penny machines. It turned out they actually cost more than a penny. My desire to go unnoticed failed. The second machine I tried hit the jackpot. For all its noisemaking and blaring lights, I won two dollars.

Deciding I'd spent enough time and money waiting to discover what else, if anything, Sarah and Maryann were up to, I sneaked back into the blackjack room. That same gambler, Maryann had been clinging to, was now on a losing streak. Maryann had at sometime released his arm and had backed away from the unfortunate guy.

I didn't want to risk taking another photo, so I turned to retrieve Ed. To my surprise, he was standing behind me, also observing. Silently, we agreed to leave the casino and compare notes.

Back in my car, Ed showed me the photos he'd taken of Sarah and the anonymous baccarat player. "I think I know what these two women are doing. They call them coolers.

I wrinkled my nose. "Coolers? Is that a new name for hookers?"

He chuckled. "Naw. A cooler is somebody who, I don't know how, but all they have to do is stand near somebody who's winning and make them lose. Lots of people say coolers are an urban myth, but I've seen things that, well, never mind. I believe that's what they're doing. And somebody's paying them to do it."

"You mean they're cheating?"

He shrugged. "There's no science to it. They even made a movie about a guy who was a cooler. Before your time. About fifteen years ago."

"Do they get paid for that by the casino?"

"Yeah. That's who would stand to gain." He rubbed his face. "Then again, maybe they are hookers."

I shook my head, wondering how to explain this to my client, Mario. Tell him his wife is either a hooker or a cooler, something that may or may not exist.

All the way back to Ed's car, my mind tried to connect this newly found information about Sarah to anything involving Pilkosky. All I knew now was that she was obviously more than just a sweet girl in love with and taking orders from Dylan Morley.

I dropped Ed off and I drove home, but I couldn't focus on anything except what I'd say when confronting Sarah. Despite my resolution not to have dinner after that chocolate cheesecake, I was hungry. I picked up a burger and fries on the way to my apartment. When I got home, though, I donated most of the meat to Charlie, who relished every bite. Absently I ate every last one of the French fries.

⁜⁝

I DIDN'T SLEEP WELL and rose at five in the morning. By six, I was on my way to the Westside Christian Center. My gas gauge was deep into Empty, so I pulled into a gas station. That's when I realized my wallet was at home. Cursing my carelessness but unwilling to return home, I dug between and under the car seats, into the cup holders and door pockets, and finally came up with six dollars in change. I quickly paid and then pumped one and a half gallons and took off to the Westside Christian Center. It was now closer to seven and I consoled myself with thinking the chances of Sarah being there were now higher.

The Center's parking lot was empty when I arrived, but I thought perhaps Sarah had parked elsewhere, on the street or even taken the bus here. I hurried to the building and checked the door. Locked. I blew out a breath of disappointment. Maybe she'd used the back entrance, especially if she was alone. I crept behind the Center, glancing left and right to make sure nobody was watching me. That door was also locked.

I shrugged, deciding to get to my office and call Corrigan with an update. I started back toward my car and almost reached the parking lot. I turned and took one last look at the Center. I spotted Sarah walking from the opposite direction and heading into the building. I wanted to give myself a congratulatory slap on the back for taking that last look.

I called to her, but either she didn't hear me, or pretended not to. She was unlocking the door and I sprinted toward her, just missing her. Luckily, I was able to stop the door from closing all the way and I made it into the hallway.

"Ms. DeNardo?" Sarah looked as sweet as ever, her blonde hair pulled back into a ponytail. Even without makeup she was lovely, her large blue eyes opening even wider in surprise.

I kept my back to the door in case I needed a quick escape. She'd already surprised me once and put me in a closet. That wasn't going to happen again. I spoke in a tone I'd use with a skittish pony. "Hello, Sarah. Sorry I startled you. I just want to talk for a few minutes. Is that okay?"

Her eyes darted to the left then the right. "Um, sure." She tilted her head to the side. "I'm really, really sorry you got locked in that closet. I just, well, I shouldn't have listened to Dylan about that. Anyway, thank you for not pressing charges against me."

It was my turn to be generous and ingratiating. "That's okay, Sarah. In fact, I wanted to thank you for making that phone call and getting me rescued."

She rewarded me with a smile sweet enough to rot my teeth. "It was the least I could do."

I returned her smile. "I was also hoping you could help

me again."

She stiffened. "You mean like testifying against Dylan?"

"No, that's definitely not it." I shook my head as if I'd just heard bad news. "I would never ask you to do something like that. What I need is to find some information about somebody. Someone who volunteered here. Maybe she still does. Her name is Maryann Wilson. Do you know her?" I pulled out the photo of Maryann her husband had given me.

Sarah glanced at it. "Um, I may have met her. Why?"

I adopted a girlfriend-to-girlfriend secretive tone. "See, her husband is afraid she's cheating on him." I showed her the picture of Maryann with the guy at the blackjack table. "What do you think? I mean, she doesn't look as if she's missing her spouse." I paused. "Are you sure you don't know anything about her or what she does at night?"

She put her hand to her mouth. "Oh, I remember now. Maryann is that woman whose husband never takes her out. She claimed she was bored and feeling neglected." Sarah shrugged. "I felt sorry for her and we went out. Just a couple of times."

I pressed my lips together, searching for a way to get her to the truth. "According to my client, you've gone out together more than just a couple of times. You and she looked like you were old pros at what you were doing." I revealed the additional pictures I had of Maryann with the blackjack gambler and ones of Sarah herself. "I'd like to give you a chance to explain."

"That's generous of you." Her sweet demeanor slipped a bit. "We're not hurting anyone."

I sighed heavily. "All right. But does Dylan know about what you're doing?"

Her eyebrows rose. "It's not as if we're selling ourselves or anything. We just help the customers have a good time. Share drinks with them. Cheer them on. But that's it. Nothing else. Besides, Dylan's in jail." She made a face. "We may never get married now. So, I doubt he'd have much to say about what I'm doing. Now, I've got to get that backroom ready for the people." She turned and headed toward the same room in which I'd first encountered her and Dylan.

I wasn't done with my questions, and I followed her. She stepped behind a folding table and started going through a pile of clothes. Her voice was steel. "I have nothing else to say."

"If he weren't in jail, would you marry Dylan now? I mean, I might be able to drop the charges against him."

She curled her lip. "We'd make a great pair. Both of us broke." Venom dripped from her tongue. "His idiot excuse for a father invested all Dylan's inheritance with that thief, Ben Pilkosky. He deserved to—" She caught herself. Her eyes narrowed and any previous gentleness vanished. "Never mind. You need to leave."

"What about Ben Pilkosky? You seem pretty angry about his handling of Dylan's money. I don't blame you. To know your chance of getting married just disappeared because of Pilkosky's greed."

She picked up a pair of sewing shears. "Leave now."

I was working on my hunch. But those blades worried me. "Was it an accident, Sarah? You didn't mean to kill Ben, did you?"

"Get out!" She waved the scissors at me and screamed, "Get out of here!"

I backed up almost through the doorway, wondering if my pistol in my purse was loaded. I kept my voice calm and coaxing. "It's okay, Sarah. I'm not the police. You can talk to me."

Her breaths were harsh and jagged, and her knuckles had turned white from clutching the scissors.

She hadn't tried to stab me. Yet. Maybe I still had a chance. "Sarah, I know what it's like to have no money. I also know what it's like when you love someone so much and you want to spend the rest of your life with them. But something or someone gets in the way. I mean, that worm Pilkosky took away your chance to be happy."

She barked, "No, you don't know. I waited four years for Dylan to come into his money and us to get married. Between that dragon, Janette, who scared him enough to make him run and end up in prison, and his father, we'll never get married." She lowered the hand holding the scissors. "Ben Pilkosky was the last straw. When I found out he'd pilfered all the money I thought I needed to get it back."

I kept my voice low, full of compassion. "What happened then?"

She was staring at the wall, talking softly, almost to herself. "I went to see him, to confront him." She snorted, "I actually thought I could get Dylan's inheritance restored." Her lower lip quivered. "I really loved Dylan and wanted to marry him. But when I asked for Dylan's money, that lowlife laughed at me. He even called me a gold digger. He grabbed my arm and told me to forget Dylan. That Dylan was a loser. That degenerate! So, when he turned his back on me, I picked up a paperweight and hit him with it. Once, twice. He went down and didn't move. I stuck the paperweight in my purse and left."

My heart was beating out a signal for me to run. I ignored it, wanting to keep her calm. "You didn't really plan on killing him, though." I needed to call Corrigan so he could get Sarah's confession. Keeping my eyes on her, as slowly and steadily as I could, I reached into my purse for my phone and my gun.

"That's good that you told me all this, Sarah. Now, we just need to go to the police and clear up this situation."

Sarah hissed, "You liar! I thought you were on my side, understood why I had to do it. You tricked me!"

I tensed and the phone slipped from my fingers. I looked away for just a moment; long enough for Sarah to raise the scissors again and lunge at me. I blocked the blades with my purse and knocked them from her grip. She pounced on me, hands around my throat. She huffed, "I didn't want to hurt you. Now, I have no choice."

Fear can make you strong. I pried her hands loose, and I pushed her away until her back was to the very closet she had locked me in earlier. We swayed back and forth, as if partners in a dangerous dance.

We were both weakening, and I feared I'd give out first. Her hands tightened around my neck again, pressing on my windpipe, blocking my airway. I couldn't breathe. In a haze, the faces of Charlie, Corrigan, and my family floated before me. My desire to live spurred me on to find the fortitude to rip her hands from my neck. Exhausted, she staggered backwards and with my final bit of power, I shoved her into the closet and slammed the door, locking it. She butted against it hard and the hinges shuttered.

I leaned against the closed door. "Sarah, it's over. The police will be here any minute now."

I pulled out my phone and was ready to call 911 when I heard footsteps rushing down the main hallway. They grew nearer. With no idea who it was, I readied my gun and ducked behind a table covered by plastic cloth.

"Police! Come out with your hands up."

My strength depleted, my breaths coming in short bursts, I laid my gun on the table and raised my hands over my head. "Glad to see you, Officer." I swallowed, catching my breath. "I'm Claire DeNardo, PI, and I've—"

The rest of my sentence was drowned out by Sarah creating a loud commotion in the closet.

The cop placed his hand on his gun. "I'm Officer Positano. Wanna tell me what's going on?"

I began again. "I'm a private detective and the person in the closet killed somebody and just now tried to kill me."

As if I hadn't told him about Sarah's actions, he asked, "You got a license to carry that gun? Lemme see some identification."

"Of course. Just reach into my purse for my wallet." My eyes opened wide and I grimaced. My wallet was safely sitting on my kitchen table. I smiled nervously. "Oh no, you see, I don't have my ID with me."

The cop's expression said he'd seen and heard it all before. "Yeah. Then let's just wait for my partner and we'll get your pal out of the closet and straighten this all up."

"She's not my pal." My voice trailed off as I spotted the other uniformed officer.

"Jeez!" The second cop shook his head when he saw me. "What's with you and this place, lady?" He turned to the first policeman. "She's a private dick. Friend of Detective Corrigan out of the—"

"Yeah, I know of him. Heard he had some wacko girlfriend was a..." He chortled. "Let's just get the other one out of the closet and get outta here."

I ignored the comment about me being crazy, but I didn't want Sarah getting away. "She confessed to murdering Ben Pilkosky, the financial advisor."

Officer Positano responded, "Until we get it all straightened out, you and closet lady are coming with us." He put his hand on the handle to open the door while the other officer kept his gun at the ready.

"Wait! Before you open that door, can I make one

phone call to clear this up?"

Positano waved his hand, "You ain't being arrested. Yet. But go ahead. Make it quick, though."

Worried that this was the day Corrigan wouldn't take my call, I speed dialed his number. I relaxed when he answered. "Brian, it's Claire. Sarah confessed to killing Pilkosky. No, I'm okay and she is too. We're here with two police officers. It seems they don't believe me."

I held the phone away from my ear until it seemed his ranting wouldn't bust my eardrum. Handing the phone over to the first cop, I smiled and tilted my head. "He'd like to talk to you."

₧₧

I WAITED IN THE EMPTY police station interrogation room for what seemed like forever. A woman gave me a cup of tea and a bag of stale chips and told me to have a seat. I'd just checked the time once more when Corrigan appeared and sat next to me.

"She confessed. Claims she didn't mean to do it. We're charging her with first degree manslaughter, although her attorney will ask for it to be dropped to second degree." He shook his head. "She asked me to tell you she's sorry she tried to hurt you. You want to press charges?"

I rubbed my neck. "Surprisingly, no. She's got enough trouble. Charged with manslaughter plus her fiancé in prison. I won't add to her problems. Besides she helped me with my new case. That should count toward me forgiving her."

Corrigan sat back. "You're in a magnanimous mood. Maybe I should ask for a favor."

"Oh? And what would that be?"

"Let me take you to dinner tomorrow night. No business talk, just us. Two normal people having a good time."

"Definitely." I smirked. "But are you sure it'll be *two* normal people?"

He laughed. It was a solid, from-the-belly sound. "Okay, maybe just one of us. I'm not saying which one, though. I'll pick you up at seven."

₮℞

I MADE IT HOME in time to watch the nightly news. Of course, that was after Charlie and I took our late evening stroll. The arrest of Ben Pilkosky's killer was the breaking news. I listened for a minute then yawned and turned off the television. I was exhausted and totally drained. Tomorrow I'd call Harold and make sure the charges against Nadia for Pilkosky's murder were dropped. For tonight, the only thing I planned on doing was dropping off to sleep.

Chapter Twenty-Five

I WAS SO DEEPLY asleep I almost missed the call on my phone. It was Harold and it was five in the morning. I rubbed my eyes. My words sounded as if I had a mouthful of molasses. "Don't you ever sleep, Harold?"

"Of course I do. When it's warranted. No time for that now, though. The charge of murder is being dropped against the client whom you know."

I yawned. "Nadia. I'm glad. What about the embezzlement charge? It's got to be clear that Pilkosky was the one taking the funds."

He cleared his throat. "Yes, it would seem so. I'm meeting with the Assistant District Attorney at ten. I'm sure everything will be settled in favor of my client. By the way, she still intends to discover who posted her bail. I have no doubt she'll be in touch with you on that."

"Sure. Fine." Another call was coming in. *At five in the morning?* "Harold, I've gotta go. Another call." This one was from Aunt Lena. Apparently nobody sleeps past four thirty. "Hi, Aunt Lena. What's up?"

"I had a dream last night."

I slouched in my bed. Aunt Lena was a firm believer in dream interpretation. "You were standing in front of a tiered cake, holding a knife like you were going to cut into it. Then, all of a sudden, your dog, Chuck—"

"Charlie."

"Okay, Charlie. He popped out of the cake, and you just stared at him, holding the knife. Anyway, he got away and that was the last you ever saw of him."

"Umm, that's interesting, but I need to get ready to go to my office."

"Wait! Don't you want to hear what that means?" She would tell me regardless of my answer, so I said, "If it's quick."

"It means Brian is going to pop the question. You know the tiered *wedding cake*? But if you wait, you'll lose him. So, make sure you say yes."

I bit my lower lip. "Aunt Lena, you see cake all day at *Cannoli's*, and maybe you were thinking about a dog or something. That dream doesn't mean anything."

She harrumphed. "My dreams always mean something. Go ahead. Don't listen to me, but when you're middle-aged and single, you'll remember what I told you. And that day isn't that far off."

"I'm only thirty-two!" I protested.

"Time passes faster than you realize. Anyway, just keep it in mind. Brian's a catch and you do love him. This time, don't let him get away. There's no third chances."

I sighed. I wasn't going to win this discussion. "Okay, Aunt Lena. Point well taken. I love you but I need to go." I ended the call and went to shower before my phone rang again.

Charlie, aka, Chuck, was anxious for a walk by the time I'd finished getting ready. I grabbed my phone and we headed out. The weather was finally reflecting mid-May. The sun was peeking out behind the morning clouds and already the chill was leaving the air. We made our way around to his favorite spot and I let him sniff around while I envisioned him leaping from a cake. No doubt he'd have eaten his way out instead.

Back inside I fed him and rummaged around for something to eat for myself. Finding nothing appetizing, I grabbed my purse, making sure I dropped my wallet into it, and a light jacket and left, deciding a bagel and tea would be perfect for the morning. I was celebrating, so I'd get a chocolate chip bagel.

Carrying my bagel and cup of tea, I got to the office. Ed was already waiting for me. Sheepishly, he handed me an article torn from a magazine. "I promised Lena I'd give you this. Don't shoot the messenger."

I took it from his hands. The feature was titled, "Why We Should Pay Attention to Our Dreams". I groaned. "Did she tell you her dream?"

Out of the corner of his mouth, he said, "Since about three this morning. Kiddo, I don't believe in dreamy stuff, but pardon my saying so, I think your aunt's dead right on this thing with Brian."

I raised my hands to block what he was saying. "At this moment, I don't want to think about it. He and I are having dinner tonight. We'll see where that leads. Now, what do you have planned today?"

He shrugged. "Thought I'd go see a man about a horse." It was his turn to hold up his hands to stop me. "Not what you think. I'm going to the racetrack. Drum up some business. We've been pretty slow."

Gratitude flowed over me for this man, my step-uncle, friend, and part-time employee. "That'd be great, Ed. Meanwhile, I'll see if I've got any budget to advertise. Fingers crossed."

He left me with the article, which I quickly wadded up and tossed. I fired up my computer to get a bit more background information for my report and then typed it up for Mario Wilson, my one client.

I finished a bit after nine o'clock, late enough to call Mario and have him come in today. I sorely needed the rest of his payment.

I reached him just as he was on break at work and he agreed to come in at noon. That done, my next dreaded task was writing up an advertising piece. I'd eaten my bagel and drank my tea and hadn't come up with anything. I decided another cup of tea would help, so I went into the kitchen to make some but a phone call interrupted.

"Claire, it's Harold Goldfarb."

"I know, Harold. What do you need?"

"It's not what *I* need, but what *you* need." Without

waiting, he went on. "I believe it would be advantageous for you to come into my office today."

"Advantageous? Why? Can't it wait until Friday? That's when we have our appointment." I didn't add that I'd hoped by some miracle to have more money by then.

"Yes, I'm aware. However this is important. Two o'clock. It will be beneficial to you, I promise."

I ran my hand through my hair. "What is it about? What I owe you?"

"Tut tut. All will be revealed when you get here."

I gritted my teeth. "Fine. I'll be there at two." When the call ended, I sighed and deleted the ad I'd been struggling with. Mario Wilson's money would have to go to Harold.

₧₧

NOONTIME CAME FASTER than I'd imagined. If time was money, it should have been moving at the speed of nothing.

Somebody was already at the office entrance. It wasn't Mario Wilson, though. It was his wife, Maryann Wilson, barreling into my office and demanding, "Are you C. DeNardo?"

I stood to answer her. "Yes, I am. Can I help you?"

She looked ready for battle. "One of the dealers at the casino called me. Mario hired you to follow me, didn't he? You took pictures for him."

I reached into my desk, ready to recover my gun, if

necessary. "That's something you should take up with him. Now, if you'll please leave this—"

She slammed her hand on my desk. "You listen to me. Mario has his nerve. Every day I cooked, cleaned and all he could do was come home, eat and watch TV until he fell asleep. That's no marriage! I wanted somebody to notice I was still attractive and desirable." A satisfied smile spread across her face. "Now he'll know. Yes, he will."

As if he'd read the script, Mario knocked on my door and I bade him enter.

Ignoring the stunned look on his face when he saw his wife, I motioned to the chair by my desk. "Have a seat, Mr. Wilson."

He moved as if I'd ordered him to step into a hot oven. Gingerly sitting on the edge of the chair, he asked, "What's Maryann doin' here?"

Maryann tsk'd, "Mario, I can hear you, ya know."

I handed him my report. "Just read this, Mr. Wilson. Then we'll all talk." I'd taken a few counseling courses in college but nothing had prepared me for dealing with this situation.

He read each page, moving his lips as he read. His bewildered look told me I needed to do some explaining. "You see, your wife isn't or wasn't cheating on you with another man. She was, um, earning money and no doubt having a —"

Maryann jumped in. "A good time. Yeah, something you don't even think to have with me anymore. We used to go dancing. Go out for drinks. Then you turned into an old man, like overnight."

Mario popped up from his chair. "That's cuz I'm tired. Earning money so we'll be able to retire and not worry."

Maryann moved quickly and was in his face right away. "Retire!? We could be dead by sixty-five! I wanna live now!"

His fists clenched. "Well, it looks like—"

I held my hands up, wishing I had a whistle. I had to depend on my voice. "Stop it, both of you. Now, I'm going to leave this room and the two of you need to discuss what's been going on like the two adults you are. If I have to lock you in here myself, I will. I'll come back when I know you can talk civilly." I stared straight ahead and made it through the doorway before they started in on each other again.

Just outside the entranceway to my reception office, Ed appeared with a guy who looked as if he weighed less than me.

Ed smiled. "Claire, I want you meet Billy Budd."

Grinning in spite of myself, I stuck out my hand. "Pleased to meet you, Mr….Budd."

The diminutive man grinned back at me. "Yeah, my mother was a big Herman Melville fan. Just call me Billy."

After we shook hands, Ed explained. "Billy here has a problem I told him you could help with. An issue with his sister."

My eyes darted from Ed to Billy and back again. "Well, I'm sorry you have a problem, Billy, but I certainly hope I can help. I have somebody in my office right now working out an issue, but how about we have a seat on the sofa here and talk."

I flashed Ed a silent thank you, and he and Billy sat on the sofa while I leaned against the empty receptionist desk.

Billy began, "My little sis, she's taller than me, but still she's my little sis. Her name's Julie. She's gotten herself mixed up with a bad guy who's two-timing her. I want you to get the goods on him so I could show her."

My insides were doing a happy dance. At last, a straightforward case that wouldn't involve murder or me risking my life.

We discussed all the details. Billy agreed to my fee and paid the retainer. I was in financial heaven.

Once we'd sorted out everything, Ed rose and slapped Billy on the back. "Come on, Billy. Let Claire do her work. I'll buy you lunch." With a quick nod, Billy rose and they both left, joking with each other.

I stuck Billy's check in my pants pocket, happy enough to face the two bickering in my office. I now had enough to pay Harold and run some advertising. My feet barely touched the ground as I prepared to patch up any physical wounds those two had inflicted on each other.

Instead of insults and fists being hurled though, I knocked and opened the door to hear affectionate banter being tossed between the two. Relief swirled with joy that they'd made up. I was smiling like a sweepstakes winner. "Sounds like everything is okay between you two."

Mario had his arm around Maryann. "Yeah, better than

okay. Maryann was right. I was getting old before my time. We both need to have some fun." He gave a wink meant only for her. "And affection."

She giggled and turned an attractive shade of rose. "Pay the lady, Babe. Then I'll show ya how much fun we can have."

For a second I thought perhaps I should have been a marriage counselor. Then I came back to reality. Mario paid what he owed me and the two re-minted lovebirds left. I hoped they'd find their happy ever after.

I added Mario's final check to Billy's. If I'd had the amounts in actual dollar bills, I would have thrown them in the air and then rolled in them once they hit the ground. But it was already twelve fifteen and I had just enough time to cash the checks and get to Harold's.

My banking done, traffic was worse than I'd figured and I was five minutes late to my lawyer's office. His receptionist, who I knew was his cousin Deborah, had me sit and wait.

Ten minutes later, Harold opened his door and bade me enter and be seated. We discussed what it would take to have my record expunged and the length of time needed. While I wasn't thrilled with any of it, I knew it was necessary and I gritted my teeth, asking him the cost of all this work.

He smiled at me, reminding me of a used car salesman trying to unload a two hundred thousand mile junker on a first time buyer. But he surprised me, saying, "Don't worry about it, Claire. I'm doing it pro bono."

I must have looked as if he'd told me he was a representative from the planet LoonyBin because he added, "Before you say anything, somebody wants to say something to you in person."

A back door to his office opened and Nadia entered the room. At first I didn't recognize her out of her prison uniform. But she grinned and rushed toward me with open arms. "Claire, thank you, thank you, thank you. I've been cleared of the murder charge and it looks as if the embezzlement charge will also be dropped. And, if it hadn't been for you," she paused and reached across to Harold, grabbing his hand. "Hank and I wouldn't have found each other."

Hank?

I opened my mouth to say something, but nothing came out. I blinked a couple of times and somehow my voice returned. "Well, I'm really glad it all worked out. And you and Harold…great. Really, great." Then Nadia informed me that Jonathan Hunt, the other partner of Pilkosky and Hunt, had just come forward and confessed to having posted her bail.

I asked, "Why did he do it anonymously?"

Nadia shrugged, "I don't think he wanted his partner to know. But I think he was suspicious about Pilkosky. Get this. He offered me my old job back." She smiled at Harold. "I may have other plans, though."

I didn't even want to pursue that topic further.

An hour later, we finished up with my business and I left, with a reluctant promise that someday Corrigan and I would double date with them.

Back in my car, I thought about the whole day. Money and love. Love and money. Today was a good day for both. I wondered if the two would continue to rule the day, especially that evening. It was getting late and I would soon be having dinner with my favorite detective.

Chapter Twenty-Six

I ARRIVED HOME to my usual greeting, Charlie jumping up and down, his wagging tail shifting his rear back and forth. I bent down and rubbed his head and then his belly, thinking how nice it was to come home to such love.

On our walk outside, I allowed Charlie to sniff to his heart's content while I ruminated on what could transpire that evening. I vacillated between excitement and nervousness mixed with a bit of dread. Not because I didn't have feelings for Corrigan. I believed I loved him and only him. Hence the excitement. But I dreaded how my life could change, my routine broken, my independence perhaps stymied a bit. Yes, I agreed to a life change when I accepted his earlier proposal. But now I was, at least in my eyes, successful. I had more confidence in my abilities, and I wanted a partner in life, not an adversary. I shook my head and forced myself to stop thinking. I'd wait to see what tonight brought and then make my decisions.

Charlie finally signaled me he had done what he had to do and was agreeable to going back inside. I obliged.

Not long after feeding Charlie and going through my mail, I showered and got ready for my date with Corrigan. I'd be lying if I claimed to be calm. In fact, the butterflies in my stomach were no match for the elephants ramming against my heart, making it feel as if it were bouncing all around my chest. Even Charlie, as if he picked up on my nervousness, danced around acting as skittish as I felt.

The knock at my door reverberated in my soul. "Claire, it's me, Brian." I could barely hear him over Charlie's barks and whimpers.

I let the man in and the moment he entered my place, all my nervousness vanished and I was grinning like one of those clown faces you throw a ball through. Then, I dazzled him with my witty repartee. "Hi."

He laughed. "Hi back." He looked me over. "You look great!" I thanked him and we both bent down to pet Charlie, nearly butting heads. I felt as if I were in some sappy rom-com.

Corrigan stood. "Are you ready to go?" I nodded and said goodbye to Charlie. Under my breath, I promised my pup if he was a good boy, I'd give him some yummy leftovers.

On the ride to the restaurant, Corrigan and I made small talk. I told him about Harold and Nadia, which had him laughing. He stopped laughing when I told him about my promise to double date with them. He shrugged. "Well, it'll be interesting at the very least."

It was so easy talking with him that it seemed we arrived at the restaurant in no time at all.

We valet parked and Corrigan took my arm. With a smile he no doubt believed to be debonair, he said, "Let me escort you, my dear."

I smiled back and we entered The Heights, one of the fanciest restaurants in town. For a second, I thought I was underdressed, but as we followed the hostess to our table, Corrigan whispered, "You're the prettiest woman in this room." My heart melted like an ice cream bar left out in the sun.

The waiter introduced himself and then took our drink order. Much as I love chocolate martinis, I decided to go with some sparkling wine. Corrigan ordered beer.

I opened my menu, but my date spoke up. "I want to congratulate you again on solving both those crimes." He shrugged. "You just flat out amazed me."

I cocked my head. "You were surprised?"

"Yeah, I was." I opened my mouth to protest, but he stopped me. "And impressed. A lot. You're good. You take chances I wouldn't agree with, but they've paid off."

I bit the inside of my cheek not wanting to say the wrong thing. *It takes a lot for me to take those chances.* Out loud I responded, "I appreciate you saying that. I know it wasn't easy."

He smirked. "No, you're right. It wasn't, but I have to give praise where it's due. And I know you work hard."

Our drinks arrived. He picked up his beer and I raised my wine glass. "Here's to Claire. A beautiful, capable woman." He put his glass to his lips but before he drank he added, "Whom I love completely."

I couldn't take a drink. It wouldn't have gone past the lump in my throat. My whisper was hoarse. "I love you too, you know."

He coughed violently and I was afraid he had choked on his beer. He wiped his mouth and grinned at me. "I'm glad we got that established."

We placed our orders, his was prime rib and mine was linguini with scallops and shrimp. My first choice had been lobster with garlic mashed potatoes, but I didn't want to risk having bad breath this evening.

The waiter left our table and brought us bread, olive oil and balsamic vinegar. Corrigan picked up a slice of bread and was tearing it into twenty tiny pieces. "Claire, I don't know how to say this exactly, but you know, you're the only woman for me. Hope you know that."

I stayed his hands or we'd have crumbs everywhere. "I know, Brian. Same with me. I mean, you're the *man* I want. But…"

His eyes went wide. "But, what?"

I removed my hand from his and swallowed hard. "I can't be with somebody who thinks my work is a joke. Or, who wants to take over what I'm doing."

He slowly wiped his hands on his napkin.

Here it comes. He's going to say it's over for us. I wanted to stick my head under the tablecloth.

"I understand, Claire. And I don't blame you for feeling that way. I know sometimes I've…doubted you. But hell, I'm a cop. I'm paid to be skeptical."

I wanted to choose my words carefully here. "Skeptical is one thing. I get that. But what I do is important and my instincts are pretty good. Actually, they're very good."

"Yeah, they are." He took a long swallow of his beer. "And from now on, I'll pay more attention to them."

My eyebrows rose in surprise. "Well, okay then."

The waiter delivered our meals, saving me from having to say anything cleverer. The smell of basil and lemon made me smile and I realized I was starving. Corrigan dug into his prime rib with such gusto I wondered when he had last eaten.

We returned to small talk throughout our meal and I was pleased when he left a hunk of meat. "I'm saving this for Charlie. I need him to put in a good word for me." He wiped his mouth. I chuckled, feeling a nice warm glow in my belly.

The waiter came over and we got a doggy box for Corrigan's leftovers. Ordinarily, I'd have a hard time passing up dessert, but I didn't think there was any room in my stomach what with the bubbles of joy filling it to the brim.

ౚౚ

WE ARRIVED AT my apartment and Charlie greeted us as if we'd been gone a decade. As soon as he caught a whiff of the doggy box contents, he went wild. I could barely get it into the kitchen and dump the leftovers into his bowl before he wiggled his way to the food.

I returned to the living room where Corrigan had already removed his suit jacket and tie. We slipped down onto the sofa and our lips had just met when my phone went off. I groaned, "I'm ignoring it."

Corrigan, to my surprise, pulled away. "Go ahead, answer it. It might be important."

I reluctantly grabbed my phone. I groaned again and answered. "Hello Aunt Lena." I made a face and Corrigan chuckled. He got up from the sofa and went into the kitchen, I assumed to see how Charlie was doing with the leftovers.

Aunt Lena practically cackled, "Okay, Claire. How did it go with Brian? You didn't mess it up, did you? Don't forget. I already bought that dress for your wedding. You have a dress too. One you can't exactly wear to work."

I harrumphed. "I remember, and no, I didn't. But a certain aunt called while he's still here. I'd call that messing up."

"Oh, okay. Got it. I'll hang up. But you call me and let me know what happens."

"I promise." I ended the call and looked around for Corrigan.

He walked back into the living room. He was smiling. "Did you give her a report?"

I shook my head. "I don't know what exactly she's expecting to happen." I noticed Charlie had also come into the room. He tried to hop up on the sofa with me, but around his neck was a ribbon with something dangling from it, which inhibited his jumping.

I looked closer at the item around his neck and pulled him up onto my lap. My mouth dropped open. It was a diamond ring, specifically the diamond ring I'd worn until Corrigan and I broke up. I looked up to say something, but Corrigan was on his knee, eye level to me. I froze. Then my mind started swirling. I blinked hard to be able to concentrate on what he was saying.

"Claire, I kept the ring, hoping that someday I'd be able to slip it back onto your finger. I didn't realize then that it would take more than time to change your mind. I had to change some of my thinking too. Anyway, I may still have a ways to go, but I'm hoping you'll help me. As my wife. Will you marry me?"

I found my voice and this time I'm sure I said, "Yes!"

———

Recipes

Fettuccini with Tuna and Tomatoes

NEXT TO PIZZA, my favorite non-dessert food is pasta. I love a good dish of bucatini bolognese or spaghetti with pomodoro sauce. Here's a dish I make, though, when I want something a little different.

Makes 4 servings.

<u>Ingredients:</u>
2 tablespoons extra virgin olive oil
4-6 scallions chopped thin (white part only)

2 (5 oz each) cans oil packed tuna
2 tablespoons capers, drained
Generous ¼ teaspoon crushed red pepper flakes
1 lb fettuccini (can use spaghetti or linguini)
1 cup sundried tomatoes, roughly chopped

Heat olive oil in large pan over medium heat. Add scallions and cook until scallions soften. Add tuna and its oil with capers, sundried tomatoes and red pepper. Heat completely.

Meanwhile, bring a large pot of lightly salted water to a boil. Cook pasta for 1 minute less than the package directions instruct. Often this is 10 minutes. Stir pasta so it doesn't stick together. Drain, keeping 1 cup of starchy pasta water.

Over low heat, add the cooked pasta to the pan with tuna mixture and stir to combine. Add some of the leftover pasta water and toss lightly until pasta is al dente (tender yet firm to the bite). Serve immediately.

Baked Chicken with Green Beans and Potatoes

WHILE I COULD EAT PASTA or pizza every day, sometimes I crave something else. This next recipe definitely satisfies that craving.

Makes 4 servings

Ingredients:

4 skin-on chicken leg quarters
2 lbs small potatoes
2 medium sized lemons, juiced, separated
½ cup extra virgin olive oil
4 tablespoons fresh basil, chopped (If using dried, cut amount in half)
2 tablespoons dried oregano
1 tablespoon ground red pepper
2 tablespoons mixed dried mustard, salt, powdered garlic, and dried thyme (Italian Seasoning
Mix can be substituted for these for a slightly different taste)
1 tablespoon white vinegar
12 oz. fresh green beans

To Marinate:
Mix the olive oil with the juice of one lemon. Add the herbs. After making slashes in the chicken, refrigerate and marinate the pieces in the oil/lemon herb mixture for 4 hours.

To Cook:
Preheat oven to 425 degrees F (220 degrees C). Grease a large jelly roll pan or a sheet with edges so nothing rolls off.

Place the chicken on the sheet. Coat the potatoes with the marinade. Once coated, arrange the potatoes around the chicken, and pour about ¾ of the marinade and the remaining lemon juice over these.

Bake in the oven for about 30 minutes, making sure the potatoes don't stick to the pan. Then cook another 15 minutes. Place the green beans in the reserved ¼ cup marinade and coat them. Remove chicken and potato covered sheet from the oven and add the green beans. Then, whatever marinade is left, pour over the chicken and potatoes.

Return the pan to the oven and bake until green beans are crisp and tender and chicken juices run clear. This usually takes another 15 minutes. Chicken should show 165 degrees F (74 degrees C) on an instant read thermometer.

Chocolate Cherry Bars

AT THE END OF ANY MEAL, be it breakfast, lunch, or dinner, I want something chocolate. The following recipe delights me in many ways. I adore the chocolate in the middle and the chips on the top. The cherry jam adds even more sweetness. Yum!

<u>Ingredients:</u>

1 cup butter or margarine, softened

2 cups all-purpose flour

½ cup brown sugar

1/8 teaspoon salt

2 3/4 cups semi-sweet chocolate chips (divided use)

14 oz. can sweetened condensed milk

1 cup cherry jam (½ cup seedless black raspberry jam instead if you like a chocolate and raspberry combination better)

Preheat oven to 350 degrees F (approximately 180 degrees C). Beat butter in mixing bowl until creamy. Then add flour, sugar and salt until well mixed. Press 1¼ cups of this crust mix onto the bottom of a greased 13 x 9 inch baking pan. Bake 10-12 minutes or until golden brown.

Meanwhile, mix one cup of the chocolate chips with the condensed milk in a small saucepan. Melt the chips over low heat, stirring constantly. Once smooth, spread it over the hot crust.

Sprinkle the remaining crust mix over the chocolate liquid. Drop the jam over the crust mix, and then add the remaining chocolate chips on top of that.

Return to the oven for another 25-30 minutes. Cool completely and cut into bars.

Acknowledgements

I OWE A BIG, BIG THANKS to my husband, Greg. Not only did he listen to my rough drafts, but also encouraged me to voice aloud my ideas, no matter how crazy. He also made a great body double! Next, I want to thank Joanne for her pep talks, her common sense, and especially her reading and feedback on my manuscript, no matter how many times I revised it. Thank you to Nancy, too, for her helpfulness and expertise at the end of it all. I appreciate Rae Dawn's input and willingness to listen to my changes and revisions, no matter how often they were done. My sister, Nikki, deserves thanks for her support and knowledge of the area in which this novel is based.

My final thank you is to the person to whom I owe so much, Kathleen Baldwin. You're an inspiration, a teacher, and a loyal friend, not to mention a great author! I don't know how I would have accomplished this book or any of the previous ones without your help.

Dear Reader,

If you enjoyed this book, please recommend it to a friend. Even lend your copy to them!

Reviews are always welcome. They help other readers discover your favorite books. If you do write one for *The Terrified Detective* series, please let Carole know. She'd like to thank you personally.

Her email is: cmsldfowkes@gmail.com

Sign up for Carole's Newsletter to get insider information, sneak peeks, contests and freebies, and to be the first to hear when her next book is coming out. Since these newsletters only come out a few times a year, you won't be inundated with them. Also, rest assured, Carole doesn't sell email addresses. The link for her Newsletter is: https://eepurl.com/8xC5L

For more information on Carole, visit her website: www.carolefowkes.com